SOUTHERN SORCERY

SWEET TEA WITCH MYSTERIES BOOK FOUR

AMY BOYLES

ONE

I happened to be standing in the middle of my little old Southern shop, Familiar Place, when all heck broke loose.

Well, it wasn't really all heck, but that's what it appeared to be at first.

The door shot open as if a great wind had pushed it. I jerked, stumbling as a swell of magic pushed me back.

The birds squawked. The kittens meowed. The puppies barked.

Hugo the Dragon fluttered up. His neck stretched forward, and his mouth opened as if ready to shoot an arrow of flame.

Oh yeah, in case you didn't know, the shop is actually a magical pet store that I own. Name's Pepper Dunn. I'm a witch who matches pet familiars with their owners.

I'll admit, I haven't been doing this witch thing for very long. I'm fairly new at it and still have tons to learn.

But it doesn't take a genius to figure out that when your front door blows open like a tornado shoved it in, you'd better pay attention.

Standing in the doorway was Rufus Mayes. In case the explosion of air didn't give it away, Rufus is a bad guy with a capital B. Like, really bad. From what I understand, he likes to play Dr. Frankenstein on folks. Once he tried to turn someone into a vampire. Or he was playing vampire on someone. Yeah, that's it.

Problem is, Rufus ain't no vampire, y'all.

He's a witch with serious issues. Four times he's attacked me—trying to take my powers or kill me or whatever. Each time I've been saved.

Anyway, Rufus wore his usual black leather from head to foot. Ebony eyeliner rimmed his eyes, and the smirk on his face told me he saw victory at hand.

"What are you doing here?" I said, pushing to my feet. "You're not supposed to enter Magnolia Cove."

"Well, here I am," he said, sauntering in. "And I don't see anyone stopping me."

My heart thundered against my chest. This was bad. This was very bad.

"What do you want?" I said.

Rufus smiled. "Why, you, of course. This time nothing's going to interfere."

His gaze landed on the animals. He shot out his hand, and the creatures fell into a slumber. Even Hugo. The dragon drifted down to the floor, falling asleep.

Last time Rufus showed up at Familiar Place, the birds attacked, sending him reeling from the store. Clearly that wasn't going to happen this time.

He looked at me and smiled. "I'm not taking any chances."

I fisted my hands. "And what makes you think nothing's going to stop you?"

Rufus raised a hand. "Because you and I are leaving."

I lunged. Rufus snapped his fingers.

Familiar Place melted away, and I was plunged into darkness.

Alone.

With Rufus.

The inky dark only lasted for a few brief seconds. An orb of light flared in the corner of my eye.

I felt a hand on my arm. I slapped it away and jerked back.

Everything righted and I found myself back in the store. Rufus stood about a foot from me. I stepped back.

"What happened?" I said.

He looked at his gloved hands. "I don't know. We were supposed to leave, but something didn't work. Drat. This always happens when I enter this cursed place. Something always goes wrong. Why? Why me? All I ever ask is to be able to work one feeble spell correctly, and I'm foiled."

He glanced at the ceiling as if speaking to whatever deity he deemed his patron saint or whatever. "Every single time. Is it too much to ask for a little magic to go my way?"

I fisted my hands. "Get out of here before I call the cops. I happen to live with the sheriff's sweetheart, so if you don't get the heck out of town, I'm pretty sure you'll be bucked out by the next ornery mule you see."

Rufus's lips spread wide as he laughed. "Do you really think I'm going to let a little hiccup interrupt my plan?"

"Well, I kinda hoped so."

His dark eyes brightened as he stared at me. "I might not be able to whisk you away from Magnolia Cove, but that doesn't mean I'm done with you."

I grabbed the first thing I could find. A telephone book. Great. I could swat him to death. This was like that horrible Facebook question where you're suddenly thrown into the zombie apocalypse and whatever item is to your left is now your only weapon.

And mine was a telephone book.

Wow. I wouldn't last five minutes against an army of zombies.

But I might be able to last a bit longer against Rufus.

I threw the phone book at him. Rufus pointed a finger at the cover, and the book shredded into confetti.

My jaw dropped.

He sauntered forward in his tight leather pants. "Since I obviously can't take you with me, at least not now, there is still another way I can get to your power."

"What's that?"

Rufus lifted his index finger and circled it. My body froze. I felt like I had been lowered into a vat of concrete.

"This is not the way to get a lady's attention," I said. "You must be a horrible person to date."

He snickered. "I don't date."

"Well not the way you act, you don't. You should be ashamed of yourself. Didn't your mama teach you any better?"

"My mother taught me the ways of dark magic."

"Not much of a hugger, was she, huh?"

That thin, amused smile was still sewn on his face when he stepped within a few inches of me.

In the past my magic has worked based on fear. It usually bolts from me, uncontrolled. All I have to do is focus on a subject and throw it out.

The problem was, I didn't feel afraid of Rufus. Maybe it was his candid smile. Maybe it was the sparkle in his eyes. Don't ask me. All I knew was the creeping fear that should have been residing in the pit of my stomach was nowhere to be found.

Traitorous fear. I nearly shook my fist in anger at it.

"Can't do anything, can you?" he said.

"That's none of your business."

I tried to focus my magic on pitching him through a window because I wanted Rufus as far away from me as I could get him.

But still nothing happened.

Rufus raised a finger and pressed it to my forehead. A zap of electricity wound over my crown and raced down my spine. My knees wobbled.

Every nerve ending in my body tingled. My fingers pulsed and my toes numbed.

"What're you doing?"

"Since I can't take you from here, and I certainly won't kidnap and hide you because Magnolia Cove is a small town, I've done the next best thing."

"What's that?" I said. My tongue felt thick; my words were sluggish.

The shop door opened. Rufus glanced over his shoulder as a customer entered. He whirled back to me, flashing a smile so devilish that Satan himself would appreciate it. Then he snapped his fingers and vanished.

My knees shot to the floor as my aunts, Licky and Mint, entered. The cats immediately started meowing, the dogs barked and Hugo whimpered.

"Pepper," Licky called out. "You in here?"

I raised a hand. My aunts flashed each other a look of fear and rushed to me.

"We just got back from a week away," Licky said.

"We wanted to check on our favorite niece," Mint added.

Licky pressed my hair from my face. "But what happened?"

Mint pulled me to standing. "You look like you've seen a ghost."

"Worse," I croaked. "Rufus was just here." I pressed a hand to my forehead. "He did something to me. Something magical, but I don't know what."

My aunts exchanged another look. Licky's mouth thinned to a line. "Then we'd better get you back to Mama's."

By *Mama*, Licky meant Betty Craple, my grandmother.

Mint thrust her shoulder under my arm. "Come on. Let's take you home." Her eyes darkened. "If Rufus is on the loose, there's no telling what he did to you. Time is of the essence."

Surely my day could only go up from here.

TWO

"*R*ufus did what?" Betty said when we arrived at the house.

I sat on the couch, a cold glass of sweet tea in my trembling hands. Hugo sat in the corner, and Mattie the Cat had come down from the bedroom to witness my crazy life.

The more the merrier, right?

I rubbed sweaty fingers between my brows. "Rufus poked me in the forehead and said that since he couldn't kidnap me, this would have to do."

Betty spat in the hearth. The crackling fire hissed in response. She waddled over to me and pushed the hair from my face. She glanced over her shoulder.

"Did y'all see him?"

Mint shook her head. "We only saw Pepper."

"She was the only one there," Licky said.

"Not even a trace of Rufus remained."

My aunts, though not identical twins, pretty much acted like it. They finished each other's sentences, and both wore their red hair long, though Mint's held gorgeous sexy waves while Licky's was bone straight.

"He snapped his fingers and vanished," I said. "Without any sort of explanation."

Betty rubbed her chin. "I could do a full-body exam on you, but I'm afraid that might not be much help. What we need is someone who thinks like Rufus. But first we also need to let the sheriff know he's in town."

Mint poked the air with a finger. "We'll do that. Maybe he'll start up a search."

With that, my aunts disappeared out the door.

Betty walked to the hearth. Above the mantle hung various dried herbs. She crushed a handful of purple flowers and threw them into the fire. The blaze turned a brilliant green before settling back to a fiery yellow.

Mattie jumped on the neck of the couch. "You thinkin' what I'm thinkin', Betty?"

Betty studied the fire before turning around and pulling her corncob pipe from her pocket. She clamped it between her teeth and lit it with a fire from the tip of her finger.

"Rufus slipped into Magnolia Cove with the intention of taking Pepper, but couldn't. Since he couldn't do that, he did the unthinkable."

Mattie blinked her brilliant green eyes. "What did the fire tell you?"

I set the sweating glass of tea on the table. "The fire? Did you ask it or something?"

Betty opened her mouth. A circular smoke ring drifted into the air before warping and disappearing. "The herbs can help me decipher things. Assist in making decisions. Here, it didn't help too much."

"That ain't good," Mattie said. "Someone as dangerous as Rufus needs to be contained, or else he'll stay one step ahead of us."

"Agreed," Betty said. "In that case we need someone with expertise in the sort of magic that Rufus works."

"What's that?" I said.

Betty's face darkened, and her voice took on an evil twinge. "Sorcery."

I shivered. "Sounds scary."

"It is, sugarbear," Mattie said. "Not to be confused with the darkest of all magics, necromancy—the raising of the dead."

I exhaled a deep shot of air. "Wow. This has gone from bad to worse."

"Not necessarily," Betty said, pulling the waistband of her jean jumpsuit to stop right below her boobs. "Magnolia Cove happens to have a resident specialist in sorcery."

I rose. "Great. Who's that?"

"Argus Amulet. And I know where he lives."

Excitement rose in me. "Awesome. Where's he live?"

"The First Witch home."

My excitement crashed and burned. "The old folk's place?"

Betty nodded. "One and the same. Let's get going. He probably heads to bed a little after noon. You know how those geriatrics are. Go to bed early, rise early."

I've bit my tongue as Betty received the senior citizen's discount everywhere she went. She would've gotten it at church if she attended.

I glanced at my watch. It was nearly twelve o'clock. "We'd better get on over there, then. I don't want my only chance to figure this situation out to fall asleep and not wake up."

I left Hugo in his cage because I figured if Rufus showed up and attacked, Betty would be just as good at fighting him as a fire-breathing dragon. I wasn't willing to bet on it, but I figured my grandmother could shoot fire from her fingertips if she had to.

Mattie, Betty and I piled into my Camry and headed over to the First Witch Center. Apparently older people didn't want to be thought of as old, so in Magnolia Cove they were called first witches, a name that I thought was pretty cool. I mean, who wouldn't want to be *first* in something as opposed to shriveled?

We arrived at lunch. The last time I'd been to the center, it was Saturday night and the witches were having Dance Night, USA, featuring crooners such as MÖtley CrÜe and Def Leppard.

No, I'm not joking.

Anyway, when we arrived, the residents were seated at tables and being served a meal of baked chicken and green beans.

"Hmm, my favorite," Mattie said.

I jerked my finger at her. "Business first. We can eat later."

"Oh shucks, sugarbear," she said in her deep Southern drawl.

Betty scanned the crowd of folks. "Let me see. Oh, there he is. Come on."

She dragged us to a table where a distinguished wizard with white hair sat at the head. He wore an emerald pinky ring that gleamed in the sunlight.

The sorcerer cut into his baked chicken with a fork and knife—very classy, if I do say so myself.

His eyes lit when he saw my grandmother. "Why, Betty Craple, what a wonderful surprise. Have you finally come to join us? Admitted to yourself that your Depends can no longer fix the leak in your brain, much less the one in your bladder?"

"Very funny, Argus. We're here on important business."

Argus forked a square of chicken into his mouth. "Hmm? Really? Now what could you ladies possibly need with an old First Wizard like myself?"

Betty pressed a hand to her hip. "It's not the First Wizard part we're interested in."

He dabbed the corners of his lips with a linen napkin. "No? What then?"

Betty placed her palms on the table, wedging herself between two women. "We're interested in the First *Sorcerer* part of you."

Argus's mouth twitched. His gaze narrowed on Betty, and then without cutting his eyes from her, he said, "Everyone, will you please excuse us?"

The other residents at the table scattered like cockroaches. I mean, never in my life had I seen old folks move like lightning—*greased* lightning at that.

Argus gestured with his non-pinky-ringed hand. "Ladies, please have a seat."

Mattie hopped in my lap. She raised her nose, getting a good whiff of the chicken, I'm sure.

Argus sliced the meat. "You wish to speak about the art of sorcery? Something I discuss with a very few privileged people?"

"Can the dramatics, Argus," Betty snapped. "You and I both know this entire town is aware of your past. Just because you talk like a gentlemen now doesn't erase what you used to dabble in."

He gave Betty a tight smile. "Then what can I do for you?"

Betty nodded toward me. "My granddaughter ran into a sorcerer today. I think he did something to her, but since my magic doesn't bend to the ways of your kind, I can't tell what."

His gaze flickered to me. "And how can you be sure, young lady, that it was sorcery you encountered?"

"Rufus Mayes walked into her store and zapped her with his finger."

Argus choked on what I could only presume was a chicken bone. He lifted his water glass and took several long sips. "Rufus Mayes? He's banned from Magnolia Cove."

"Tell him that," Betty spat. "Someone, somehow let him in. We've notified the police, but that doesn't change the fact that he touched my granddaughter and I want to know what he did to her."

"So do I," I said. "Please, Mr. Amulet, if you can help me, I would be forever grateful."

"Forever is a very short time to me, my dear," he said.

I nearly rolled my eyes. Yes, I knew he was old and he wouldn't live for another ten years or so, probably, but hey, he could still show a little respect for my thankfulness.

Sheesh. Some people.

With a feeble hand Argus clasped the cane resting beside the table. He pushed his chair back and rose, leaning on the instrument.

"Ladies, come with me."

We followed Argus out a side door into the gardens. It was peaceful, with only the chirps of songbirds interrupting the silence.

"The Werewolf War of '52 is how I got my bad leg. It's stayed with me ever since," he murmured as we passed a hibiscus with bright pink petals.

"Werewolf War?" I said.

"Yes. Most of my kin fought in the faction that won. I was lucky enough to be among them, though I didn't get away scot-free. Lost my leg. The synthetic one that replaced it isn't quite as good, but I've gotten used to it over the years."

"Was there a bombing or something? Is that how you lost it?"

A rich, velvety laughed escaped Argus. "Of course not, my dear. I was attacked by a sorcerer. His spell killed my leg, though it spared my life. It was a small price to pay for a beating heart."

"I agree," Betty said. "An arm or a leg is nothing compared to a life."

Argus's eyes glinted with something—more amusement, maybe. "Though some might disagree. The government didn't. They thanked me for my service."

We reached a shack behind a large elephant ear bush. Argus poked in his pockets until he found a key. He unlocked the door and gestured for us to step inside.

The *shack*, as I had referred to it from the outside, was nothing like that on the inside.

The bulbs buzzed with electricity when Argus snapped them on. Crystals of all colors were immediately illuminated. Red and yellow, azure and teal, lavender and onyx—the entire room was filled with them. Some sat on shelves, others were suspended from twine that dangled from the ceiling, while others were set in statues. A stone gargoyle stared at me with ruby crystal eyes. I shivered.

Competing for space on the shelves next to the crystals were what I could only think of as talismans. These were shapes constructed of iron or steel, with feathers and rocks attached to them. They came in circles and triangles, pentagrams and squares. Even though the designs were simple, there was something intimidating about them.

In fact, the entire room seemed to hum with an undercurrent of energy. One corner in particular stole my attention. It was a rack of shelves lined with clear vials. In the vials were colored powders, eyeballs, feathers, bones—an assortment of organic substances that I could only figure were used in the art of sorcery.

"What in hell's bells is this place?" I said.

Betty swatted me.

"What?"

"The cursing. No granddaughter of mine curses."

I rolled my eyes. "I don't consider hell to be a curse word. When it's a place as well as an expression, it's PG."

"Says you," she huffed.

"That's exactly right," I said smugly.

"Ladies," Argus said, "this is my retreat from the sterile halls of the center. It's where I come to remember who I am." He ran his fingers down one of the feathers hanging from the ceiling. It was gigantic, as if it had fallen from a whale-sized bird.

"What is that?"

"A griffin tailfeather."

My jaw dropped. "A griffin?"

Argus's lips twitched in amusement. "Yes, my dear. I am a collector of many things, including magical creature elements."

Mental note—do not let Argus near Hugo.

"I don't harm the creatures, of course. I only take something if they're willing to give, otherwise the magic wouldn't work. Not my magic, at least. There are others who trade in creatures. That's not me."

"Yes, I know all about people trading in creature parts."

Just yesterday I'd helped solve a case involving dragon bloodstones. In fact, I had found myself on the wrong end of a gun. If it hadn't been for Axel Reign, my kind-of boyfriend, I wouldn't have survived at all.

Argus shook a finger at the feather. "That particular bird was instrumental in assisting with a spell I was working on. Unfortunately she became wounded. She had a nest, and I brought food to the babies. To repay me, she offered a tailfeather. I've never had a reason to use it."

Argus gestured for me to stroke it. I slid my fingers down the orange and brown spots. It was silky and soft. "Amazing. What can you do with it?"

"Oh, a variety of things. It can be a tonic that helps other magical creatures; it could potentially stop time, though I don't know for how long or if the world would be stable enough to actually handle such a thing."

"Amazing," I said, mesmerized.

Betty shuffled between us. "Yes, all of this is wonderful, Argus, but we're here for a reason. Time might not've stopped, but it's certainly wasting away while whatever bug Rufus gave my granddaughter goes to work."

"Yes, yes, Betty," Argus cooed. "I haven't forgotten why we're here. Your granddaughter clearly has an interest in my workroom. I was only explaining a few things to her. No harm. No foul."

Argus caned his way over to a bench and sat. He motioned for me to join him. I did, feeling more like a patient in a doctor's office than a witch about to be inspected by a sorcerer.

"My talents may be a bit rusty," he apologized.

Betty crossed her arms. "The only thing rusty about you is the bit of red growing under the handle of that cane. Your talents are as good as they were half a century ago, Argus. There's no reason to pretend they aren't."

He chuckled softly. "Aren't you confident?"

"I am. Always will be. It's the Craple in me."

Argus placed a soft, warm hand over mine. "Close your eyes, my dear. Let me take a look and see what I can see."

I closed my eyes, though I was tempted to peek. Argus placed a palm to my forehead and hummed something.

"Ah, yes. Ah. Tell me, when Rufus touched you, did you feel something?"

"Yes, it felt like energy zipping over my head and down to my feet."

"But it didn't hurt," he said.

"No. It only felt strange."

"I see." He released his palm. "You may open your eyes."

13

Betty padded forward, throwing a shadow over me. "Well? What is it? What did that scoundrel do to her?"

Argus grabbed his cane and cradled both hands over the silver handle. "It appears as if Rufus has cast a bonding spell on your granddaughter."

Betty's lips pursed so far they disappeared. After a moment of casting Argus with the stink eye, she said, "What sort of bonding spell?"

Argus leaned away, resting his back on a row of shelves. "From the looks of it, it appears as if whenever she uses her power, it won't work for her, but instead will fuel Rufus."

I gasped. "He said he wanted my magic."

"And that's how he plans to own it," Argus said, rising. "Whenever you work your power, it will go to him, essentially rendering you powerless."

"So he'll own my magic?"

Argus nodded. "That is correct."

I shot Betty a concerned look. At that moment I felt an ache bloom at my temples. That was bad. Very bad. Axel had explained to me that as a head witch, I had to blow off my power every once in a while.

And a headache was always the first sign that I needed to work some magic.

I brought my fingers to my lips but resisted the urge to gnaw on them. "If I don't own my power and it goes back to Rufus when I use it, that means I won't be able to purge the excess, which means my magic could kill me."

Argus swiped a finger beneath his bottom lip. "I'm afraid, my dear, that you are correct."

THREE

"What am I supposed to do?" I said frantically. Part of me wanted to rein in my panic and play this cool, but that part of me didn't win.

Betty studied Argus. "Do you know a way to stop the spell?"

Argus riffled through his vials, blowing dust off a few and tapping the clear glass. "Perhaps. It will take some time for me to work up the proper spell. It's a tricky job, reversing such complex magic." He chuckled. "Rufus is nothing if not creative and imaginative."

My hopes, though they didn't crash and burn, certainly petered out a bit. "When do you think you'll have an answer for us?"

"Oh," Argus said, eyeing the green, goopy contents of a particularly revolting-looking vial, "return the day after tomorrow. That should give me plenty of time to decipher what I need to do. This may require dusting off a book or two."

"We'll return then," Betty said.

This was one of those times when I wished Axel was here. Unfortunately, last time we'd spoken, he said that work would take him from town for a few days.

Of course work would take him away when his soothing voice and smile would be two things guaranteed to lift my spirits.

Betty and I followed Argus out, where we were met by a young man in a suit. He was tall with sandy hair that he swept out of his green eyes with a shake of his head.

"Granddad, I've been looking all over for you."

"My dear Samuel, when at first you don't succeed, try, try again." Argus turned to us. "Ladies, meet my grandson, Samuel Amulet. He visits me nearly every day and is more concerned with my well-being than is natural."

Samuel punched his hands in his pockets. "My grandfather looks innocent enough, but he tends to stay in trouble around here. I like to check in, make sure he's walking the straight and narrow."

"And how narrow do you think he's going to do that with a Sorcerer's Shack out here?" Betty said gruffly. "There's enough magic buzzing in those four walls to blow the roof right off Magnolia Cove."

Samuel eyed her questioningly. "The town doesn't have a roof."

Betty fisted her hands on her hips. "Youngster, if I say this town has a roof, it has a roof."

"I wouldn't argue with her if I were you," Argus said. "Betty Craple practically runs this town."

"As I said," Betty said proudly, "if it weren't for me, Magnolia Cove would implode."

Mattie started off toward the main complex. I tugged Betty's jumpsuit. "I think we've disturbed Mr. Amulet enough. We have our answers. Thank you," I said to him. "We'll be back day after tomorrow."

"Yes," Argus said.

Samuel waved. "I didn't catch your name."

"Pepper Dunn."

He took my hand the way a Southern gentleman is taught, by holding it as if he would raise my hand to his lips. But instead he only gave a slight wag.

"Pleasure to meet you," he said.

"How do you do?" I replied.

Feeling his green eyes burn into me for a little too long, I pulled my hand away and turned toward Betty.

A young blonde nurse exited the main center and greeted us. "Mr. Amulet, ready for your physical therapy?"

"My dear," I heard Argus say as we slipped inside, "if you're the one massaging my leg, I'm ready for anything."

With that, the three of us left the First Witch Center and headed to the car.

"I know you're worried," Betty said as she fastened her seat belt, "but Argus is the best sorcerer around."

"What about Axel?"

Betty's gaze slashed right and left. "Do you see your boyfriend nearby? Because last I checked, he was out of town. Plus, he's a wizard, not a sorcerer. He may know a thing or two, but when it comes to combatting Rufus's skill level, we need wisdom, not beauty."

Mattie curled up on Betty's lap. "Thank you, I know I'm beautiful."

I laughed.

Betty pulled her pipe from a pocket and slid it between her teeth.

"You're not going to smoke in here, are you?"

"I was thinking about it."

"I prefer if you wait until we get home. Some scent won't come out of the fabric."

"That's the least of your problems from the look of this old car. Besides, you're already risking old person smell just by having me in here."

I cranked the engine. "I wasn't going to say that."

"No need." She took a long puff and exhaled. "I'll just pretend I'm smoking. Helps me think better."

I steered us back toward downtown. "What are you thinking about?"

"Obviously the second most important issue that's occurred today."

"Which is?"

"How the heck did Rufus Mayes manage to get his butt back in Magnolia Cove?"

"Right." I eased on the brake as we reached a stop sign. They didn't want to work, so I pumped them a few times until the brake fluid finally lubricated the joints enough to stop.

Betty shot me a worried look. "Is this thing safe?"

"You smoke a pipe, which could give you cancer, and you're asking if my vehicle is safe?"

"It's a valid question."

Once the intersection was clear, I pressed the gas. "It's safe enough. The whole brake thing is a new problem. I'll see if Axel can check it out when he returns to town. But anyway, you were talking about how Rufus got in."

"The spell used to ban him was created by three people—me, Barnaby Battle, who's the new mayor, and Sylvia Spirits, who owns the witch hat store."

"Witch hat store?"

"Yeah. It's a controversial item. Sylvia says the hats amplify your powers, make you a stronger witch."

"Well? Does it work?"

Betty exhaled a pretend puff of smoke and then watched what would have been rings dissipate in the cabin.

"You've seriously got a problem," I said.

"I like my pipe. When you get to be my age, kid, it's the little things in life that bring happiness."

I smirked. "It's already the little things in life that bring me happiness. Anyway, so what do you want to do? Visit Sylvia?"

Betty nodded. "Take a left on Wishing Well Road. Her shop's at the corner of the next residential street."

I stopped the Camry in front of a green cottage with white shutters. It was late summer, and encore azaleas bloomed bright pink on either side of the door.

The wood shingle sign in front of the cottage read CHARMING CONICAL CAPS.

"That's a mouthful," I said.

Betty unclipped her seat belt. "As I explained, it's more for advanced witches than a newbie, and even then many magical sorts don't buy into it."

I tapped the steering wheel. Glancing at my chipped polish, I realized that boy, I sure could use a manicure. Perhaps there was a magical store in town that would do such a thing. In fact, if I asked, I was bound to find one.

"But if Sylvia was one of the three of you who created the spell that kept Rufus from entering, she must be a powerful witch."

"Oh, she's one of the best, that's for sure. But the whole hat thing isn't for me."

"Why not?"

She smiled secretively. "You'll see."

We hopped out. Mattie stretched her back legs. "Y'all, I'm gonna head back home if you don't mind. I've had enough ridin' around to last me a week."

"Nap time?" I said.

"You got it, sugar."

Mattie padded off as Betty and I made our way to the cottage. I let her lead, unsure if a hat would pop out and attack me on entering.

Hey, crazier things have happened.

Like today with Rufus, for instance.

When she opened the door, hats of all shapes and sizes greeted us. Some sat on mannequin heads while others were draped over pegs. Several were propped on hat stands, and a few hovered in the air, about head height. They bobbed and spun in gorgeous pinks, ivory, citrine, onyx, emerald, lime, lavender, aquamarine. I swear, Sylvia covered every color of the rainbow with her hats. If you needed one to match an outfit, you wouldn't be disappointed.

"Greetings," Sylvia said, gliding over.

Like many of the female residents of Magnolia Cove, Sylvia Spirits had red hair. Hers shimmered cherry red and hung straight, parted directly in the middle. Sylvia wore a crimson mermaid-shaped gown, and she slithered over the floor as if sliding on rollers.

I was immediately intimidated, to say the least. Most of the other shop owners that I'd met were regular people. They weren't extras from the cast of *The Addams Family*, as Sylvia seemed to be.

She air-kissed both my grandmother's cheeks. "Betty Craple. What a wonderful surprise." She stood about a foot taller than my grand-mother, though Sylvia made bending to kiss her appear effortless. They parted and her gold eyes landed on me. "And this must be the granddaughter that the entire town has buzzed about."

I gave an embarrassed wave. "Pepper. How do you do?"

"Very well, thank you."

"All these niceties are great, but we've got a serious problem, Sylvia."

Sylvia waved the air dismissively. "Yes, yes, I'm sure. But first, why don't you take a look at my newest collection?" She slid over to a row of pointed hats in autumnal colors. "Fall will be here in a few weeks, and to prepare for Halloween, I've created a new conical that's guar-anteed to amplify any holiday spells you might make."

"Conical?" I said.

"The shape of the hat," Betty said behind her hand. My grand-mother rolled her eyes.

"Got it."

Sylvia took a beautiful nut-brown hat from a peg and placed it on my head. "This would look absolutely wonderful on you. Try it out. Give it a whirl."

"Sylvia, she can't," Betty said. "That's why we're here."

Sylvia's eyes widened. "Oh?"

"Rufus got in."

"Impossible," she hissed. "Rufus Mayes? You must be mistaken."

Betty shook her head. "I am not mistaken. He attacked my grand-daughter this morning, placed some sort of spell on her."

"But I didn't feel any breaking or thinning of the spell."

Betty cocked an eye at her. "Are you sure?"

Sylvia opened and shut her mouth. "No. Yes. I'm positive. Come. Let us see."

She tapped a wall lined with hats. The wall swung back, revealing a dark room. Inside, a bubbling cauldron with icky yellow liquid bubbled and boiled.

Sylvia grazed her hand across the opening and shut her eyes. A rainbow of light shot up from the center and then crashed back down, hovering over the cauldron. It looked like a miniature galaxy. It was amazing.

"What's that?" I said, totally mystified.

"That," Betty said proudly, "is the spell that keeps Rufus locked out of Magnolia Cove. At least it was."

Sylvia studied the lines and circles, the dots and swirls. "Nothing appears to be wrong. Everything's in place, but you say he got in?"

Betty drummed her fingers on the lip of the cauldron. "He broke in and, as far as I know, is still here."

"I don't see where the spell has been tampered with," she said. "Every line is perfect."

Betty frowned. "If it has been messed with, that can only mean one thing."

I tucked a few strands of crimson and honey hair behind my ear. "What?"

Betty's lower lip trembled. Oh crap, it had to be bad if her lower lip was acting that way. I never, and I mean never, saw her in any way, shape or form, reveal the tiniest hint of vulnerability.

The shinola had finally hit the crap fan.

When Betty spoke, I held my breath. "That spell was fine-tuned to Rufus's body, the magic inside of him. He couldn't have broken it."

Sylvia scraped black-tipped nails down her face. "It can only mean that someone helped him." She stopped and took a moment to stare at the two of us in turn. "Someone inside Magnolia Cove found a way to sneak Rufus inside. Someone's working with him."

FOUR

"*B*ut who? Who could be helping Rufus?"

The three of us sat at a table in the back of Sylvia's shop. She'd poured us cups of coffee. Luckily I had a stash of jelly beans in my purse ready to plop into the bitter liquid.

Sylvia shook out her mane of hair. "That, I don't know. It's the sort of information the police will have to drag from him."

I glanced at Betty. "Speaking of that, maybe we should see where they are in their search."

"Good idea. Sylvia, thank you for the coffee."

Sylvia nodded. "Pepper, are you sure you wouldn't like to try on a hat?"

I shook my head. "No thanks."

"Now's not a good time," Betty said.

Sylvia walked us to the door. "Let me know if there's anything else I can do."

When we got inside the Camry, I turned to Betty. "So where are we headed?"

"To the police station. I want to see how Garrick's getting along in his search for Rufus."

I cranked the engine just as a horn blared outside. It sounded like a tornado siren—a sound I'm all too familiar with living in the South. In the springtime sirens blare in cities at the first whiff that there's a twister nearby. It's a good thing, too, because Alabama is practically its own tornado alley.

"What's that?" I said.

Betty smirked proudly. "Just listen."

The siren died, and a voice boomed from behind it. "Citizens of Magnolia Cove. You are currently under lockdown. Please leave your places of business and go to your homes. Close the doors and windows. Do this now."

"Garrick's voice," I said.

Betty nodded. "They're looking for Rufus. They haven't put the town on lockdown in years. They mean business. Come on, let's get home and see what's going on."

"Why don't they just tell everyone to stay where they are?"

Betty snorted. "Tell a bunch of witches they can't go to their homes where they're safe and sound with their cauldrons and potions? That would never fly in this town."

It took a few extra minutes to reach the house as folks spilled from their businesses, jumped on their cast-iron skillets and flew off. We had to wait as pedestrians crossed in front of us. A few cars piled up. Not many folks drove in Magnolia Cove, so the small traffic jam was a first to see.

Anyway, when we reached the house, Mint and Licky were there, along with my cousins, Amelia and Cordelia.

"Why are we on lockdown?" Amelia said. "Our mothers wanted to wait until y'all got here before they told us anything."

Licky flicked her hair over one shoulder. "We just didn't want to rehash it a thousand times."

"There's only two of us," Amelia said, pointing to Cordelia.

Mint crossed one leg over the other and bobbed it up and down. "We often have to spoon-feed the two of y'all every little bit of information."

"I resent that," Cordelia said. She glanced at Betty. "What's going on?"

"Rufus is in the town," I said. "He attacked me this morning. Well, not in a punch-and-knife sort of way, more of in a sneaky I'm-going-to-steal-your-powers manner."

Amelia and Cordelia exchanged glances. "So did he steal your powers?"

"No, but apparently he cast some sort of spell so that when I work magic, he absorbs it. He did say he wanted to get my powers, after all."

Cordelia nibbled her bottom lip. "And I guess he planned on getting them."

Betty turned to my aunts. "What happened at the station?"

"Well," Mint said, "that nice new sheriff we have, that Garrick, didn't want to listen to us as first."

I frowned. "What do you mean?"

Licky snapped and a nail file appeared in her hand. She sawed at the edge of her fingers as she spoke. "Well, you know, with the whole Cotton and Cobwebs fiasco, I guess he thought we were a little, you know, loopy."

My aunts, caring as they may seem, are actually chaos witches. Pretty much wherever they go, chaos and destruction follow. In fact, I wasn't sure how keen I was on having them in the house at all. I wasn't in the mood for dealing with a caved-in roof. Not that they could help it. It was just the nature of their magic.

"But he eventually listened," Cordelia said.

"Interested in what your boyfriend's doing?" Betty snarled.

Cordelia rolled her eyes and didn't respond.

Mint pulled her hair over one shoulder. "He listened. Got his men looking."

"Garrick knows about Rufus's history," I said. "Garrick was here when the council voted to allow Rufus inside for his mother's funeral, so it shouldn't have been too big a deal for him to get his men moving."

"But we are talking about our mothers here," Amelia said.

They shot her dirty looks.

"No offense, but you don't exactly have the most respectable reputations around town."

"I resent that," Licky said.

"We're the ones who caught Mayor Peter Potion," Mint added.

"If it weren't for us, that old guy might've killed Pepper," Licky said.

That was true. Not long ago my aunts had saved me from near death at the hands of the town mayor.

"Yes, yes, you're heroes," Betty said. "So they've got us on lockdown, which means someone else must've spotted Rufus."

I cracked the knuckles on my right hand. "Why do you say that?"

"Because your aunts headed to the police station before we had a chance to speak to Argus."

"Oh, we stopped for ice cream first," Mint said.

I rubbed the worry line wedging its way between my brows. "Nice."

"Betty's right," Cordelia said. "Someone else probably did see Rufus, which means they're closing in on him."

Amelia brushed her hands as if ridding them of dirt. "And then they'll just toss Rufus out and throw away the key."

"Wait," I said. "They can't toss him out."

Betty waddled over to the ever-burning fire in her hearth and tapped the empty cauldron with her finger. The bowl immediately filled with water. "He cast a spell on Pepper. We need Rufus here." She shot Mint and Licky a dark look. "You did tell Garrick about the spell, right?"

Mint grimaced at Licky. "We told him, right?"

Licky clicked her tongue. "I'm pretty sure we did."

"I almost remember doing it."

"I'm nearly one hundred percent positive that you mentioned something about the spell," Licky said with confidence.

"Oh, I thought you were the one who mentioned it," Mint said.

"No, it wasn't me. If either of us said anything, it was you."

"I thought I heard it come out of your mouth."

I clenched my fists in frustration. "Will one of you please just say if you told him?"

"I didn't," Licky said meekly.

"Me neither," Mint said.

I bit back the geyser of panic rushing up my throat. I held the fear roiling in my stomach at bay as I studied Betty. "They didn't tell Garrick. What does that mean?"

Betty scratched her chin. "It can only mean one thing—that as soon as Garrick catches Rufus, he'll send the sorcerer on his way."

I took a deep, cleansing breath, hoping for the best outcome before ·I asked, "But what does that mean for the spell?"

Betty pulled at the silver, curled wig covering her head and said, "Why, it means we'll never be able to break it if they let him go."

I grabbed my purse and rushed to the door. "Come on. We've got a sheriff to catch."

FIVE

*A*s soon as we stepped outside, I saw several police officers on cast-iron skillets zoom overhead.

"Grab your skillet, Pepper," Betty said. "We're going on a chase."

I ran inside, grabbed my long-handled skillet that was meant for one thing and one thing only—riding high in the sky. I rushed back outside. "Where's yours?" I said as I hiked a leg over the handle.

"I'm riding with you."

Oh boy.

Now the only other being that had ridden with me was a cat I liked to refer to as Sweetie Death Wish, but who's real name had turned out to be Sprinkles.

And Sprinkles had weighed a heck of a lot less than Betty Craple, who was mostly head and boobs.

I cocked a brow. "How exactly is this supposed to work?"

"I'll get on the back and hug your waist. It'll be easy, and don't worry about the extra weight. I'll cast a spell that makes me light as a feather."

"Oh? Can you cast one like that on me? Except make me lose ten pounds?"

She shuffled up behind and wrapped her arms around me. "Doesn't work like that."

"Okay, five then? I'd settle for five pounds."

"No."

"How about you just get rid of the love handles on my sides."

"What love handles? Kid, you weigh what I weigh and you've got love handles that keep on giving."

I settled onto the tip of the cushioned skillet. "I don't want those kinds of handles."

Betty took up the very back of the seat. "Neither do I. Hurry or we'll lose them. Fly this thing."

I focused on lifting off— "Wait! What about using my magic and powering Rufus?"

Betty smacked her lips. "Right. Move your head to the left. I'll fly this thing from behind."

And so she did. And did she ever. Betty lifted the skillet and zoomed up into the sky, giving me a healthy mouthful of bugs along the way.

I spat out something that I didn't want to analyze. "Gross."

"You should've worn goggles," she shouted.

"I don't have any."

Suddenly a pair of goggles rested over my eyes. "I need a mouth guard."

"No can do," Betty yelled. "Goggles are all I can manage at the moment. Gotta focus on the trail."

"What trail? I don't see any police."

Half a second later a green line of smoke traced the sky in front of us.

"Did you do that?"

"No, the Easter Bunny did."

"I don't see an Easter Bunny, only an old witch with a wig who likes to smoke a corncob pipe."

"Very funny. Yes, I did that. We're following their trail."

We zipped over oaks and pines, magnolias and dogwoods as we

flew across town. I glanced below. The houses melted away on our path to the Cobweb Forest.

The trail of green smoke disappeared into the thick woods.

"Hang on," Betty said. "We're going down."

We punched through a hole among a copse of pines and settled on the ground, where we found ten police officers, including Garrick, had surrounded Rufus Mayes.

Rufus dragged his gaze from the police officers and studied Betty and I with his dark eyes. He smirked as if he'd just won the lottery.

"Come to tell your dogs to go home?" he said, referring to the cops.

I jumped from the skillet.

Garrick flashed me and Betty a scathing look. "What in the world do y'all think you're doing here?"

"You can't send him away," I said.

"I can and I will," Garrick said. "Men, take him to the barrier."

"No," I shouted, jumping in front of the line of men. I didn't know where this barrier was, and I wasn't sure if it would affect me, but worse things could happen than receiving an electric jolt.

I mean, hadn't they already? I was freaking tied to Rufus Mayes, a dude who had made no bones about the fact that if I didn't go with him on certain occasions, I would die.

Actually I was beginning to think that was a bluff. After all, he couldn't use my power if I was dead, now could he?

"Pepper, if you don't move out of the way right now, I'm going to arrest you," Garrick said.

Betty nearly poked Garrick with her boobs. "Then you'll have to arrest me, too, Officer, and boy, you'd hate to have me in jail. I'm pretty sure I'd need someone to dig the dirt out from under my toenails."

Garrick rolled his eyes.

I flared my arms wide. "Seriously, you can't send Rufus away. He cast a spell on me. A spell that connects my magic to his. Anytime I use my power, it gives him strength."

Garrick narrowed his gaze. "A spell?"

"I'm not lying. Trust me, I want him gone more than you know. I wouldn't be here otherwise."

Garrick turned to Rufus. "Is that true?"

Rufus opened his arms as if in surrender. "It's as the lady says. I've cast a joining spell on her. What she does fuels me."

Garrick squinted at him. "Are you freely admitting you sneaked into Magnolia Cove illegally and then worked magic on a resident?"

Rufus smiled. "It is true."

"Then I have no choice but to arrest you."

Rufus lifted his palms. "Arrest away."

Garrick nodded to one of his men. "Rufus Mayes, you are under arrest for working magic on a resident of Magnolia Cove. Until such time as you are sentenced, you will be placed in jail. Do you understand?"

Rufus smiled as an officer shackled a pair of glowing handcuffs to his wrists. "Oh, I understand indeed."

The officers dragged Rufus through the forest. Rufus shot me a smile that made vomit creep up the back of my throat. "It looks like I won't be going home, after all."

Garrick crossed to me. "I don't know what you're thinking, pulling a stunt like showing up during a lockdown and arrest. For goodness sake, at the worst one of us could've blasted you with magic."

I folded my arms. "And at the horrific, which in my opinion is a thousand times worse than the word 'worst,' you could've sent Rufus back to be free in the world, and I'd be tied to him for the rest of my life."

Which, unless Argus figured out how to break the spell, could be very short given the fact that my headache hadn't dampened one iota.

"Well, just be sure to stay out of trouble," Garrick said.

"Don't worry. I plan on it."

Garrick followed the trail of officers as they climbed on board their skillets. They placed Rufus on his own, but then magically roped it to another officer's ride, so that he couldn't get away.

Rufus smiled at me as they lifted up into the trees and disappeared in the green canopy.

I kicked a pinecone on my way over to Betty. She held the skillet with one hand and scratched her chin with the other.

"Something's not right, is it?" I said.

She dragged her gaze from the men. "Hm? What? Oh, I don't know. I was just lost in my thoughts."

"I'll say it again, then. *Something's not right.* The way Rufus is acting, it's almost as if he wanted to be arrested."

"That's what I was thinking."

I dug my fingers into the worry lines sprouting on my forehead. "Now I'm worried. Not that I wasn't before, but I really am now. If Rufus's plan was to be arrested, I have a bad feeling he wants more than just my magic."

Betty nodded. "That makes two of us. Rufus Mayes may have big plans for Magnolia Cove."

"Big bad plans."

"Ones that involve you."

I climbed on the skillet. "Then what do you suggest we do?"

Betty rubbed her chin. "I say we have some dinner, 'cause I'm starved, and then we head back over to Argus, see if he's found anything out."

"But he said to give him two days."

I glanced over my shoulder. Betty pulled out her corncob pipe. "Yes," she snapped, "I'm going to smoke and ride. I hope you don't have a problem with that."

I shrugged. "If you're talented enough to make that work with the wind blasting your face, then I'm impressed. But anyway, about Argus —what if he's not ready?"

Betty's face hardened. "Argus won't have a choice but to be ready. The safety of every citizen might be riding on him."

SIX

*D*inner was a quiet, somber affair. Even the meal itself seemed sad—limp turnip greens, black-eyed peas and ham hock with more hock than ham made a scrimpy supper.

Mint and Licky hadn't stayed around, and Amelia and Cordelia pushed their food around their plates with their forks. What was left of the ham bone I gave to Hugo, who gnawed it greedily on a newspaper laid out on the kitchen floor.

"If I've got to sit here with a bunch of whining and complaining babies, I'll be happy to throw every one of you out," Betty snapped.

My cousins and I exchanged confused glances.

Cordelia jabbed a pea. "What are you talking about? We're sitting here."

"It's the *way* you're sitting here," Betty said, slathering butter on a cornbread muffin. "Y'all are sitting here like the world's ending. Like you're contestants in a moping contest to see who wins by getting the most mopes."

"I don't think 'mopes' is a word," Amelia said.

"And you," Betty snapped. "You're the worst."

Amelia frowned. "I'm the worst? We're all worried about Pepper and this stupid spell, and I'm the worst? What am I doing?"

A spark of fire lit in Betty's eyes. Oh crap. I didn't know what was coming, but I knew she was goading Amelia for a reason. I was just afraid to find out exactly what that was.

"You've been complaining about your job for days."

Amelia shook her head. "No, I haven't."

"She hasn't," Cordelia added.

Betty leaned back in her chair and studied Amelia. "You can say you haven't, but I've heard your silent cries for help."

Amelia's grip on her fork tightened. "I don't know what you're talking about. I love my job."

"Filing?" Betty said.

Amelia sniffed. "I'm good at it."

Betty snapped her fingers, and a magical rolodex appeared.

"Not this again," Amelia said. "I thought after the last catastrophe you were going to stay out of my love life."

"This isn't about your love life."

The rolodex shot a beam of light upward like a projector. An image appeared of a woman in a chef's hat stirring something in a ceramic bowl.

"What's that?" Amelia said.

"I'm trying to find you a new job."

Amelia shook her head. "But I don't want a new job."

"You might want this one."

Betty shuffled through the rolodex again. Images whizzed by until she stopped. The picture on the screen showed a vault and a man with a key.

Amelia's eyes widened. "Oh, what's that?"

"I thought you weren't interested in a new job," Betty said smugly.

"I might be interested in that one. What is it?"

Betty crossed her arms and looked very proud of herself. "Magnolia Cove has an opening for a Vault keeper."

"Vault keeper?" I said.

Cordelia folded her napkin. "The Vault keeper helps guard the town's riches, whatever those might be. Potions, jewels, whatever."

Amelia tapped her fingers together. "Oh, that sounds fascinating. Would I get to see what's in the Vault?"

Betty nodded. "Probably."

Cordelia yawned. "Sounds boring."

"But I'd get to file things, wouldn't I?"

Betty nodded. "I'm sure there would be all sorts of categorizing for you to do."

A spark lit in Amelia's eyes. "And I could file the town's secrets."

Betty pushed her chair back. "More or less. You'd know secrets, but of course you'd have to be discreet."

"Oh, I'm discreet."

"Think about it. I can get you an interview if you're interested." Betty nodded toward me. "You ready to track down an old man?"

I cracked my knuckles. "I'm ready."

Truthfully I was a bundle of frayed nerves. I'd wanted to call Axel, let him know what was happening, but I didn't want to worry him. I figured by the time he got back, all of this would be over. I'd be free of the spell and Rufus would be on his way back to whatever hole he'd crawled out of.

I crossed my fingers that things would play out exactly like that. Was I asking for too much?

I certainly hoped not.

Betty and I drove over to the First Witch Center. A nice lady greeted us when we entered—it was the same nurse from earlier in the day. She had short blonde hair cropped to the neck and a pink barrette clipping it on the side. She had full lips and an easy, friendly smile.

"We're looking for Argus Amulet, Delilah," Betty said.

"Ah yes," she said. "Argus went outside after supper. Said he needed to work in his shop. I believe you'll find him there."

Once she was out of earshot, I said, "You know her?"

Betty sniffed. "It's a small town."

I followed Betty along the path lined with elephant ears, hibiscus and other plants that made me feel I was in the jungle more than I was at First Witch Center.

We reached the shack, and Betty knocked. No answer.

"Maybe he went back into the center?" I said.

She mumbled something about people keeping a closer eye on the residents and marched back inside. We found Delilah quickly.

"He's not in there. Maybe he went back to his room?"

Delilah smiled pleasantly and nodded like a bobblehead doll. "His room is 105, right down the hall."

I followed Betty to his room. The door was open, with no sign of Argus.

Betty frowned. "I don't like the looks of this. Let's go back to the shack."

I tucked a strand of hair behind my ear. Frustration started building inside me, but I followed her without a word.

She knocked again at the shack.

I grabbed the knob. "For goodness' sake, let's just go in."

Moving like geriatric lightning, Betty threw her body across the door. "You can't enter a sorcerer's domain without their approval."

"Well, we can't exactly wait forever for Argus to show up. What if he fell asleep? Betty, he's my only hope of getting rid of this spell."

I grimaced.

She studied me. "The headache getting bad?"

I nodded. "I need to use my power to get rid of it, but I can't while Rufus is attached. We don't know what it will do. Feed him? Drain the lifeblood from me? I don't plan to find out because behind that door may be a sleeping man—one who can solve this problem."

I gently brushed her aside. "And if you're too afraid to go in, I'll take the wrath, whatever that may be."

Betty poked a finger in my shoulder. "Even if that giant feather attacks you?"

I hesitated, but deciding there was no other choice, I said, "Even if that giant feather attacks me."

With that, I turned the knob and slowly pushed the door open. It was unlocked, and I was pretty sure that Argus wouldn't leave it unlocked unless he was inside.

The lights were out and the room was dark, but I saw a shadow slumped on the bench.

I glanced over my shoulder. "He's just asleep like we thought."

I padded inside with Betty directly behind. A skylight allowed slivers of light to pierce the darkness.

"Mr. Amulet? Sorry to intrude, but my grandmother and I were hoping you'd been able to crack that spell. See, we think something bad's going to happen, that Rufus is up to something that could affect all of Magnolia Cove."

The figure didn't move.

"Mr. Amulet?"

I reached out and touched his shoulder. Mr. Amulet fell to the floor.

I jumped back. "Holy shrimp and grits!"

Argus Amulet's sightless eyes gazed upward. Rubber tubing was tied around his arm, and dangling from his skin was a syringe.

"Well," Betty said, stepping forward, "it appears our best hope of getting you out of this mess is now dead."

I crumpled to the floor beside Argus. Betty was right. Argus was dead, and unless my luck changed, I might be right behind him.

SEVEN

"*L*ooks like Argus injected himself with a healthy dose of deadly nightshade," Garrick said.

We stood outside. Even though the humid night was warm, a chill settled on my skin, making me shiver.

"Deadly nightshade?" I said.

He lifted a bottle in a plastic bag. The label read DEADLY NIGHTSHADE.

"Oh," I said. "I guess it's obvious then."

"Sorcerers often use the stuff to achieve a trancelike state," he explained. "It can help them see whatever it is they need, meaning it assists in contacting the spirits."

"So it basically works like LSD?" I said.

Betty glared at me. "How do you know about those sorts of drugs?"

I shrugged. "I know it's a hallucinogen. I imagine that's what the nightshade does."

Garrick nodded. "But he dosed himself way too large for that."

I rocked back on my heels. "You mean you think this was intentional?"

"That's what it looks like."

I raked my fingers down my cheeks. "There's no way. Argus was helping me. He was trying to break the spell that Rufus cast. He wouldn't have killed himself."

Garrick's lips thinned to a line. He wrapped a hand on my shoulder and said, "He was an old man, and I'm sure one in a lot of pain. There's no evidence of foul play. Maybe it wasn't suicide. Could've just been an accident, but there's no way to know. Argus is gone and won't be able to help you."

I glanced at Betty. "What do we do now?"

She tapped her foot impatiently and glared at Garrick. "That's an excellent question. What are we supposed to do now? You're holding Rufus because of a spell he cast on Pepper. How long can you detain him?"

Garrick glanced at the ground as if thinking. "A couple of days, tops. But I need evidence of a spell; otherwise I'll have to escort him out of town. Makes people uncomfortable having him here. No one's said anything, but I can tell. They don't like him."

I twisted my hair over one shoulder. "We need someone else who can help us."

"I might be able to assist."

I glanced over my shoulder to see Samuel Amulet coming out of the shack.

He shook hands with Garrick. "Thank you for everything. It's horrible to see Granddad like that, but he did like his nightshade. Used it a lot to get him into the state he needed to help connect with the other side, or whatever."

"I'm sorry for your loss," Garrick said. He tipped his ten-gallon hat to us. "Ladies, if I can be of any help, let me know."

He left Betty and me alone with Samuel. "What was my grandfather helping you with?" he said.

"A sorcerer cast a joining spell on me. I need it broken."

Samuel grimaced. "Boy, that is a hard one. That's a real pickle, I tell you what."

I shot Betty a concerned look. *Pickle?* I hadn't met many sorcerers, but they seemed more mature than to use the word *pickle* in the context of me being permanently chained to Rufus for the rest of my life.

"Follow me," he said.

Samuel led us into Argus's shack. The body had been removed, but having found Argus dead in there, I had the creeps just standing in the room.

Samuel started sifting through the shelves. "There's a labradorite stone here somewhere. That rock holds tons of magic. Lots of power."

Betty poked me in the ribs. "It's well-known in town."

"The stone?" I said.

"Oh yes," she said, nodding. "One time—and I have to give credit where credit is due—Argus used that labradorite to stop a giant turtle from eating all the vegetation down at the potion ponds."

I cocked a disbelieving brow. "A giant turtle?" I mean, how big could a turtle get?

"Oh yes," she said. "That sucker weighed a good two tons. A nasty witch out of Hickory Hollow sent it up because she said Melbalean Mayes had cursed her petunias so they wouldn't bloom."

"So she conjured up a giant turtle and sent it to devour the entire town of Magnolia Cove?"

She patted me proudly on the shoulder. "Granddaughters of mine are pure geniuses. Yes, that's exactly what happened."

I rolled my eyes. "Okay, anyway, what can this orb do?"

Samuel stopped digging through the shelves. "It holds power from deceased sorcerers. It can help. One of the most powerful magical objects around. Been in our family for years."

He stopped searching and stood glaring at the shelves, a deep frown embedded on his face. "But right now it doesn't appear to be here."

"Don't know where it is, huh? Your granddad didn't trust you with it?" Betty said.

"He did trust me," Samuel said. "I am an Amulet. I have just as much magic as my grandfather ever did."

"But you don't know where the orb is," she said.

His jaw clenched. "I will find it. And when I do, I will come to your home and destroy whatever magic this two-bit sorcerer has done to you. Don't worry. I'm every bit as capable as my grandfather ever was. More so."

"Hmmm. Too bad you can't just use some magic and figure out where the labradorite is," Betty said.

"I will find it," he shouted.

I cringed and tugged Betty toward the door. "Let us know when you do. In the meantime we'll be around. You won't have any problems finding me."

Betty and I left.

"His grandfather didn't trust him with the labradorite, did he?" I said to her.

"Nope," she replied, "and if we want to get you out of this mess, we'd better start looking somewhere else. Otherwise you'll be connected to Rufus for the rest of your life."

I rubbed the ache in my temples. However long that would be.

WE GOT home and I went straight to my room. Hugo was nestled in his cage. I let him out and played with the dragon for a few minutes. Mattie lay curled up in the window seat.

"That sorcerer figure out how to cure you?" she said.

"He's dead. Committed suicide with deadly nightshade."

"What?"

I shrugged. "Either that or it was accidental overdose."

Mattie blinked at me and stretched. "I don't believe that for one minute."

"I have a hard time with it, too, but that's what all the evidence points to."

"Don't you find it suspicious that Rufus shows up and then the one man you need to help you *against* Rufus winds up dead?"

I stopped in mid-tug of pulling my pajama pants up one leg. "What are you saying?"

"I'm sayin', sugar, that I think the whole thing smells worse than rotten fish in a barrel."

"Is that a thing?"

"No. But it would be to a cat. We love fish."

I laughed, but I thought about what she had said. I gnawed the inside of my cheek for a moment. "You think Rufus is responsible for Argus's death?"

Mattie stretched. "Don't you think Rufus would know who the one person was that you would seek out to help you? Rufus is from here, after all, and he's a powerful sorcerer."

I considered that. The police had found Rufus this afternoon. There's was no telling how long Argus had been dead, but the nurse at the center seemed to act as if she'd seen him recently, which wouldn't work because Rufus had been caught much earlier.

"I don't know. I'm not sure it adds up. They caught Rufus hours ago. Argus was found recently."

Mattie sat on her haunches. "A sorcerer like Rufus can do all sorts of things. I don't think his involvement can be written off so quick. Sugarbear, don't you think Rufus wouldn't want anyone to suspect him? He could've done something to the nightshade. Perhaps he made it more poisonous, knowing that Argus would use it."

I rubbed my chin. "That sounds feasible. So I guess I let Garrick Young know about all this in the morning?"

Mattie yawned. "Girl, if you want any kind of truth, I suggest you go talk to Rufus yourself."

I nearly fell over. "What? Talk to him? About what? And do you really think Rufus is going to admit anything to me? It's not as if he's going to say, 'Well, of course I poisoned the old man. I didn't want anyone to help you.' He's not going to do that."

Mattie winked at me. "He might."

This cat had more than a simple conversation up her sleeve. "What're you talking about?"

"I'm talkin' 'bout the fact that you go in there and play to Rufus, let him think he's in control, and he might slip up. That fool may tell you exactly what he's plannin'. What he wants. And he might just break the spell. I mean, you ever even had one conversation with him?"

I shook my head. "No. And I don't want a conversation with him. I don't want to talk to him. Mattie, he's tried to kill me. You saved me from him back in Nashville. Why would I put myself at risk and go talk to him?"

"'Cause you might be able to discover a secret about the spell he cast on you. That's one thing."

"What's the other thing?"

"I don't know. I haven't figured that out yet. Heck, I'm only a cat. I cain't do everythin'."

I lay back on the bed. "I wish Axel was here. He would know what to do."

I heard Mattie thump to the floor and pad over to the bed. She jumped up, landing softly. "I'm sorry about Axel. Have you called him?"

I shook my head. "No. I don't want him to worry."

"Listen, instead of being all mopey, why don't you get dressed? I'll go with you to the police station. I'll distract whoever's on duty, give you time to talk to Rufus. What do you think?"

I dug the heels of my hands in my eyes. What did I think about that? Worst-case scenario, nothing would happen. Best case was that I would find out some nugget of information that could help.

I sat up and glanced at the gray cat staring blankly at me. "All right. Let's get down to the station."

Not wanting to be caught by Betty sneaking out of the house, I decided stealth was the way to go. So I grabbed my skillet from a corner in the room, threw open my bedroom window and crawled up onto the roof. I hiked a leg over the handle, and Mattie jumped onto the pole, balancing as only a cat could.

We flew through the quiet night, and I landed softly outside the station.

Mattie jumped off. "You wait here."

I leaned the skillet into a knot of bushes. "What're you going to do?"

"I'm going to jump on the desk and grab something that'll really tick off the officer who's on duty. Maybe his keys. Then I'm going to run out the front door and keep him busy for about ten minutes."

"How're you going to get in and out of the door?"

Mattie blinked at me. "Why magic, of course. I can open a door if I need to."

I nodded appreciatively. "Wow. I'm impressed. I didn't know you could do that."

"Sugarbear, I'm not just a pretty face. There's lots I can do."

I hid a laugh behind my hand. "As you've proven."

"Okay, now get ready."

I waited across the street while Mattie wiggled her way inside the station. I held my breath as she stayed out of sight for several seconds.

Suddenly the glass door flew open. Out ran Mattie, keys dangling from her mouth. An officer rushed out behind her.

"Get back here," he yelled as he ran down the street.

This was it. My big opportunity to talk to Rufus. I exhaled a deep cleansing breath, clenched my fists and crossed the road, ready to face my enemy.

EIGHT

$\mathcal{I}$ didn't have a watch to keep up with the ten minutes Mattie had promised me, and I also didn't know what to expect from Rufus.

The one thing I can say for sure is that I walked in and found Rufus standing alone in the cell with his arms outstretched and fingers wrapped tightly around the bars.

He smiled when he laid eyes on me.

"Nice distraction."

I shrugged. I needed to look strong, not like the wiggly wimp I felt inside.

Wait. Why the heck did I feel like a wimp? That isn't how I was supposed to feel. There was supposed to be an undercurrent of anger residing beneath my anxiety and fear.

I tested out my gut, probing around. Yes. In the midst of my trepidation, a smidgen of fear resided.

Y'all, I needed that fear to face down the man who currently smiled at me as if he ran the world. I had to yank every bit of confidence and anger I had from the depths of my core and use them just to look him in the eyes.

I sauntered in, thrusting my shoulders back and raising my chin as

44

if, come heck or high water, I would win at this little game of cat and cat. I refused to be a mouse.

"You like the distraction? All my idea."

But any advantage I could use, I would.

His dark eyes danced with amusement. "Clever."

I stopped in front of the cell. Rufus's gaze dragged from my feet to my crown. "To what great pleasure do I owe your clandestine visit?"

"Quit it with the big words. Just talk to me like a regular person."

He released the bars and rose to full height. "Fair enough." The amusement in his face extinguished. "What do you want?"

"Whatever it is you hope to achieve by tying me to you, it won't work."

"Oh? Isn't it already?"

"No. There's someone working on breaking the spell. By tomorrow, your link to me will be severed, and you'll be on your way back to whatever hole you crawled out of."

He quirked a brow. "Can you be so certain?"

I crossed my arms. "Yes. I can be so certain."

He smirked. "Really? Because as I see it, the first person you would've run to would've been Argus Amulet." He clicked his tongue. "And what a shame, but I hear he's dead. Quite dead. In fact, so dead that I don't think anyone will be able to bring him back."

"Not even you?"

He chuckled. It was a deep, rich, velvety sound that sent a wave of shivers racing down my spine. "So you've heard the rumors about me."

"Rumors? From what I hear, they're fact."

"Fact can be misconstrued."

"Playing vampire on someone can be misconstrued? Not sure how that works."

He turned away and glanced around his cell. "You think this is it for me? You think what I do, I do for my own selfish needs?"

"Seems like it."

"Tsk, tsk, Pepper Dunn. What I do isn't for me. It's for the rest of the world. I am a pioneer."

"You're not wearing a hat and riding a wagon. Those were pioneers. This isn't the Wild West, and you're not a cowboy. So no, I'm pretty sure the last thing you are is a pioneer."

"Not that sort of pioneer," he sneered. "What I do is for witches and wizards everywhere."

"So you're misunderstood. Is that it?"

"The work I perform may not be understood for a very, very long time. But believe me, it's cutting edge."

There was something about his dark eyes—how they speared me. A flame of intensity and even sensuality wafted off Rufus. Probably it was only the connection between us and not something more. But if Rufus approached a young woman and asked if he could suck her blood, I could see where it would be very easy to say yes.

Something truly mesmerizing lay in his eyes. That simple knowledge sent a sliver of ice straight to my heart.

"Did you kill Argus? You know about his death."

Rufus laughed. "No. Why would I kill him?"

"So that he couldn't break the connection between us. If one even exists."

His eyes narrowed to slits. "So you don't think it's true."

"No," I said, bluffing.

Rufus held up his palm and blew into it. Tendrils of magic floated in the air toward me.

"Of course most of my magic has been neutralized. Everything except what's between us."

Magic curled toward me.

"Push it back to me," he said.

I twitched my head. Surely such a small use of magic wouldn't do much for him. But would I be able to control it? The only times that I'd ever really used my magic effectively—other than being scared to death, that is—was when Hugo had been around.

What the heck? Might as well try.

I pressed my fingers to my throbbing temples and shoved the magic back to him.

I felt a snap, like a rib cracking in my chest. It didn't hurt. It was like popping a very large knuckle.

He smiled. "You felt it. Oh my dear, that connection is very real. Incredibly real. What I could do with your power if you just surrendered it to me. Let me warp and use you."

"Use me how?"

Rufus balked. "In ways. Ways I can't tell you about because they're top secret."

I crossed my arms. "You don't know what you're going to do, do you?"

His face reddened. "Of course I know what I'm going to do. I just don't want to tell you because, well...things. Reasons. I have them. That's for me to know and you to find out."

I rolled my eyes. "Okay. Well, I see this isn't going anywhere."

I turned to go.

"The labradorite."

I stopped dead. I looked over my shoulder. "What did you say?"

He smiled again—part snake, part seducer, and all sorcerer. "I said the labradorite."

I frown. "What about it?"

"It's gone missing, hasn't it?"

I lifted one shoulder in a half shrug. "I'm not sure."

He smiled wickedly. "Of course it has. Otherwise you'd already be free of me. Or would at least be partway there."

"So that's the key?"

"Is it?"

I slapped a hand to my thigh. "Listen, I am getting real sick and tired of you answering a question with a question. I know you're up to something, I don't know what but I know you're in here for a reason. You wanted to be caught. I can't prove it, but I feel it in here," I said, pointing to my chest.

"In your shirt?"

"No. How can you be so dense? In my heart. I feel it in my heart that you conned someone into letting you into Magnolia Cove, then you spelled me and probably killed Argus and made it look like a suicide."

"Now that," he said sharply, "I didn't do. A real sorcerer always takes credit for what he's done. And that wasn't me. Find another murderer, if that's what you're looking for. Otherwise I'll be here, waiting for you to simply surrender to the bond between us."

I threaded my fingers through my hair. "Because once I surrender, what?"

He shivered as if the thought was the most pleasurable idea ever. "Once that happens, your power will be mine, and then the only thing that will limit my abilities is my own imagination."

"Or your own sanity."

"That, too." A confused look flashed over his face. "Wait. I don't think that came out right. Anyway. Surrender, Pepper. Do that and everything will be so much easier. For you and Magnolia Cove."

I rocked back. "You are here for a reason other than me."

His face fell. "I don't know what you're talking about."

Feeling a surge of confidence, I strode up to the bars and grabbed them. "That's it, isn't it? You're here to do something to the town. With every breath I have, I will find out exactly what that is."

Suddenly it sounded as if an explosion came from behind me. I whirled around to see a cloud of dust filling the space where the front doors had been.

Had been.

That's right. Past tense. The doors were gone. Blown away by some sort of force.

I coughed and waved dust from my face. For a moment panic filled me. Was this someone come to break Rufus out?

Then a shadowy figure strode forward. Long, strong thighs crossed the room in less time than it took for my heart to empty of blood on the downbeat.

My knees shook when I saw the dark look on his face. Fear rocked my soul as Axel walked to the cell and raised his hand.

Rufus slammed against the concrete wall. He groaned.

"That's for entering Magnolia Cove," Axel said.

"Daring," Rufus wheezed.

He pushed himself off the floor and dusted his black leather pants.

Axel gripped the bars of the cell so hard I swore I heard the metal start to bend. "What I'm going to do to you for screwing with Pepper will have to wait until they release you."

Rufus chuckled. "Ah. Is the *beast* upset with me?"

"If I could let the beast rip you to shreds, I would."

Rufus sneered. "How do you know you can't?"

The way Rufus watched Axel gave me the creeps. There was some twinge of truth in his words.

After all, it had only been a couple of days ago that Axel had fought his twin brother, Adam. During the fight, both men had started shifting into their werewolf forms. Before that, I had believed Axel only changed during the full moon—one night a month.

Afterward Axel couldn't explain why or how the shift had started. Luckily it hadn't been completed.

Axel snickered, turning away from Rufus. For the first time his gaze met mine. He strode over to me, heat blazing in his blue eyes. Axel cupped his hand under my head and pulled me to him for a deep kiss. The motion startled me, but only for like half a second. Then I was curling my fingers into his T-shirt and inhaling the wonderful scent of musk and leather that drifted from his skin.

When he pulled away, Axel tipped his forehead until it touched mine. "We're going to get you out of this. If I thought killing him would help, I'd do it."

I laughed nervously. I didn't know if he was kidding, but I didn't feel his words were far from the truth.

"It's good to see you, too," I said huskily.

He grazed his calloused fingers across my cheeks. "I came as soon as I heard." He kissed my forehead and threaded his fingers through mine. "We'll find a way out of this."

"Think you've got the chops to break what I created?" Rufus said.

Axel's face twisted into a dark expression. "It wouldn't be the first time. You don't own the rights to magic, Rufus, and there are much better and more educated sorcerers in the world than you. I happen to be one of them."

"We'll see, beast."

Axel stiffened. He released my hand and crossed back to Rufus. "You won't see anything. You'll be stuck here, rotting in a cell until they kick you to the curb. So no, you won't see how you're defeated, but you will be. And when I do solve your little spell, I'll personally take you to the boundary." He lifted a finger. "I promise you, that's one trip you won't want to take. So remember that. Sleep with it and let it fill every second of your thoughts. Because when you see me again, it won't be a charity call."

Rufus raked his gloved fingers through his black hair. "Whatever you say, beast. Whatever you say." Rufus's eyes widened. "Looks like it's time for y'all to go."

I heard the distinct sound of boot heels on the tile floor. "Do one of y'all want to explain what tornado flew through my station?"

I turned around to see Garrick Young standing in the open doorway, the glass doors broken behind him.

"I just happened to walk by and saw this mess. What happened to my man?" he said.

I cringed. "I think he was distracted. He should be back soon."

Axel pointed to the doors. "That's my fault. I'll fix it."

Garrick scowled. "I know you're ticked about this situation, but you can't destroy police property. You and I go way back, Reign."

Axel ran his fingers through his hair. "I'll fix it. Then we'll get out of your hair."

Garrick nodded. "Sounds like a solid plan."

Axel kissed my cheek. "Wait for me outside. This will only take a minute." He raised his arms as I scampered across the room, darting around Garrick and hoping his scowl couldn't hurt me in any way, shape or form.

When I reached the threshold, I glanced over my shoulder, catching one last glance of Rufus. His dark eyes probed mine, and he shot me that unwinding, curling smile that sent a shiver of fear straight to my heart.

Yes, he had a plan that was bigger than the connection he'd made to me. Of that, I was certain. But what I didn't know, was how to stop him.

Thank goodness Axel was back. As soon as I had him alone, we'd make a plan to defeat Rufus.

Or at least I hoped to heaven and back that we could, because I had a feeling Magnolia Cove had no idea what was coming. Since I didn't know what to expect, I also didn't know how to stop it.

NINE

*M*attie ran up as soon as I stepped outside. "I think I lost him, sugar. You get what you needed?" Her gaze swept to the broken doors and Garrick and Axel. "Oh, well, it looks like you might've gotten more than you bargained for."

I grimaced. "I think you're right."

Mattie licked her paw and rubbed one side of her whiskers. "Since you don't need me anymore, I'm going on home."

"Are you sure you don't want a ride?"

"Oh, I'm sure, honey. You and Axel probably got a lot of kissin' to do."

I rolled my eyes. "Okay. Well, I'll see you at the house."

"Sounds good."

With that Mattie disappeared into the night. A few moments later the police officer who'd chased her appeared, took one look at the doors and started cussing.

I quietly excused myself to a row of trees in the distance, where I watched Axel fix the doors in a storm of power that looked more like a lightning shower than magic.

It was pretty cool, y'all.

He marched outside with a purpose and intention I'd never seen in him before. I have to say, it was incredibly sexy and stirred my hormones in a way that I knew to be dangerous.

Best to stay far, far away. After all, if Betty could sense when we kissed, who knew what else she could sense?

Something I didn't want to find out, thank you very much.

Axel wrapped a hand around my neck and gently kneaded his fingers into the rope of muscles. "Are you okay?"

"I'm fine, but Axel, I have a feeling that whatever Rufus wants isn't going to stop at me. There's something strange about everything. I mean, the police didn't have too hard a time tracking him down and nabbing him."

He cocked his head. "He could just be stupid. To spell you the way he did suggests it."

I poked his chest. "It's not that. There's more to this than just me."

Axel took my hands and stopped, studying me. The bloom of intensity in his eyes made my lower lip tremble. "I don't care about the part that isn't you. I care about you. As soon as Garrick called to tell me what was going on, I returned. I'll do whatever I can to break this spell. First things first, we need to speak with Argus Amulet."

I shook my head. "Don't you know? He's dead."

His eyes flared. "Dead?"

"Tonight. Shot himself up with a lethal dose of deadly nightshade."

"Not Argus."

"Yes, he did. Killed himself."

Axel exhaled a deep breath. "I've known Argus a long time. Consulted with him on several cases. He knows how to dose that stuff. He wouldn't have committed suicide."

"I confronted Rufus about it, because let's face it, he's the most likely to have killed Argus, but he didn't know anything. Not that he would tell me the truth, but I thought at least he might reveal a nugget of information."

Axel released my hands and raked his fingers through his shoulder-length dark hair. "I'm still digesting what you told me about Argus. No way he killed himself. No way." He glanced at me. "And it was nightshade?"

"Garrick has the vial."

"Okay, there are a lot of cogs going in this thing. Do we know how Rufus was able to enter Magnolia Cove?"

I shook my head. "No."

He clicked his tongue. "So even if we kick him back out, he could still reenter. We need to know that won't happen. Next, I need to work on getting you separated from Rufus."

I rubbed my temples. "Could you make that sooner rather than later?"

Concern slashed across his face. "Why?" He then glanced at the starry heavens as if asking for a bone. "The headaches?"

"I've had one all day."

"Let's get that solved, then." He took my hand again. "Come on."

"Where are we going?" I said.

"To Argus's shack."

"At this hour? You're kidding."

He shook his head. "Not kidding. We've got to break that spell."

"But it's probably locked."

Axel smiled. It was the first time I'd seen him do that since he'd blown the doors off the police station. "I know where he keeps the key."

～

WE REACHED the First Witch Center a few minutes later. Axel had driven his truck, and I hopped in after I stored the skillet in the bed.

"Are we going to get in trouble for sneaking around the center at night?"

Axel drove with one hand on the wheel. He tipped his face toward me. "I don't care if we get in trouble. We're investigating a potential murder of a good friend of mine."

I nodded, sinking back into the bucket seat. A wave of sadness filled me. "I'm sorry. I didn't know you were close to him."

"Seems like that's just how it's been going lately. I was close to your uncle, too."

"I know."

Axel had helped out my Great-Uncle Donovan quite a bit before he passed away. In fact, Axel had shown me things about my store that I wouldn't have learned otherwise, simply because he and Donovan had been so close.

The pickup rolled through town, eventually coming to the center. Most of the lights were off except those illuminating the foyer. We parked and Axel killed the engine.

"We're going around back."

"With all that dense shrubbery? Won't there be spiders?"

His lips coiled into a grin. "I'll protect you. How does that sound?"

"By going first and breaking all the webs?"

He nodded. "Exactly."

I slid from the seat and quietly shut the door. Axel came around and threaded his fingers through mine. He guided me around back, speaking softly as we walked.

"It's against my better judgment to have even brought you."

"Why?"

He glanced over his shoulder. "Because I'm trying to keep you safe."

"Well, I'm not exactly a wilting flower. In case you haven't noticed, I'm not going to sit at the house and wait for you to fix this."

"I've noticed," he said sharply.

I pulled my fingers from his. "What does that mean?"

We'd walked around back and were facing the dense foliage. "It means you have a knack for finding trouble."

I crossed my arms and didn't move. "I know you're not saying I was asking for Rufus to do this to me."

"Of course not." He sighed. "All I'm saying is, I want to keep you safe. I probably shouldn't have brought you, but I did."

"If I'd known you were coming, I would've insisted in going with you."

"That's what I mean. I can't keep you away from trouble."

I scoffed. "It's not as if it's your job to keep me *from* trouble. I can take care of myself."

He shook his head. "Why is this suddenly an argument? I want to keep you safe, but obviously I can't."

"But it's not my fault."

His voice rose. "I didn't say it was your fault."

"Well, that's how it sounded."

"You're making something out of nothing."

"No, I'm not."

He rubbed his forehead. "Listen, would you stop arguing and just come with me so that I can figure out how to break the spell?"

"And do what? Save a damsel in distress?"

His lips curved. Axel took a solid step toward me until only a slip of air passed between us. "Is it so wrong to want to save you?" His fingers brushed a strand of hair from my cheek.

My nose twitched. I bent my ankle, letting my foot roll over in nervousness. "No. You can save me anytime you want."

"That's what I was hoping for." He took my hand. "Come on and stop back talking. We've got work to do."

As much as I didn't want to, I couldn't help but chuckle at his comment. "If you didn't push me to it, I wouldn't back talk."

Axel shot me a dirty look over his shoulder. I blinked innocently at him.

We reached a part of the garden that the lights from the building couldn't penetrate. Axel seemed to know his way by heart, or possibly it was scent from the werewolf part of him that led him effortlessly to the front door of Argus's shack.

A ceramic frog sat to one side. Axel gently tugged off the head and retrieved a key from the porcelain belly. He slid the key into the lock, and a moment later the door swung wide.

I followed him in, and he quietly shut the door behind us. Axel opened his palm, and faint light glowed in the center.

My eyes flared. "Some trick."

He wiggled his eyebrows. "I'm full of surprises."

"So I see."

"This way we won't draw attention to ourselves by flipping on the light." He walked silently around the room. His lean form stirred something deep inside me.

Axel and I had experienced a few ups and downs in the short span of time that we'd been involved. In fact, that sucker had broken up with me a few days ago—for my own protection, it had turned out. It had been a rough couple of days without him. Watching him now, I understood part of that.

The guy was hot and the chemistry between us, sizzling.

But it was more than that. I kinda "got" Axel and Axel kinda "got" me. It was cool. A lot of mutual respect ran between us. But even still, we were moving slowly through this. The last thing I wanted was to rush into a relationship that neither of us was ready for.

But watching him now, I can tell you that I was just about ready for anything when it came to Axel.

Better not tell him that.

He moved to a collection of stones and started picking them up one by one. "No labradorite."

I cocked my head. "Samuel, Argus's nephew, mentioned something about that, too. Said he needed the labradorite for the spell." I leaned on one hip. "And you know what? Rufus said something about it, too."

Axel swung around and faced me. "What did he say?"

"He guessed that it had gone missing. How he knew, I have no idea. But once again it makes the whole thing look like Rufus had a hand in Argus's death."

Axel swept the light over a wall. "It's a very precious stone and happens to be what I need to help you. Now whether or not Argus was going to use it, I don't know, but it probably would've been in his arsenal."

"Samuel seemed pretty ticked it was gone."

"I can understand that."

"Why?"

Axel dusted off a container and looked inside. "Because Argus didn't have any faith in his grandson's abilities as a sorcerer and Samuel knew it. Always irritated him. There's nothing worse than the one person you respect thinking that you'll never live up to their standards."

I twisted a strand of hair absentmindedly. "Yeah, I can see that, but I didn't get that sense from Argus."

"He was very polite. At least, most of the time. It's not something he would've told a stranger."

"Are you looking for something other than the labradorite?"

"Ah," Axel said, "here it is."

I walked over and glanced at his hand. In it lay a small twisted lump of feathers. "What's that?"

"It's something that can help with what Rufus has done to you. At the very least it may be able to ease the pain of your headache." He grabbed a thick black tome with a cracked binding. "And I definitely need this."

"And that is?"

"An arcane spell book. Lots of secrets in here. In fact, I wouldn't be surprised if the very spell Rufus used lay hidden inside somewhere."

I shoved my hands in my pockets. "It would be amazing if that were the case."

He handed it to me, and I hugged the book to my chest. "What else do you need?"

"That I won't know until I'm in the thick of things. And I'm hoping I don't need the labradorite, because that could be a problem."

Unfortunately something told me that he might need it, which would mean we were possibly up crap creek without any sort of paddle.

"And one last stop." Axel opened a cabinet with glass doors. He pushed aside vials that tinkled and clanked as he worked. "This is where Argus kept his nightshade, among other potions and elixirs he might need."

"Oh? Why're you looking in there?"

Axel pulled out a vial. "This is why."

He presented a bottle with the word NIGHTSHADE.

"I don't understand. There was already one bottle found with that in it. The one Argus used to kill himself with."

58

Axel's mouth tightened. "That's my point. Argus only ever kept one bottle of the stuff at a time in here. For safety purposes."

I pressed at the worry lines creasing my forehead. "So what you're saying is that the other bottle labeled 'nightshade' wasn't his?"

Axel nodded. "Right. It wasn't and I'm going to prove that Argus was murdered."

TEN

*A*xel took the few items, and we slinked from the shack, heading back toward the pickup.

"Did you find the labradorite?"

The voice popped out of the darkness. I shrieked, throwing my hands into the air. Axel pushed me behind him in a protective stance.

"Who's there?" Axel said.

Samuel Amulet shuffled from the bushes. "Well? Find what you were looking for?"

Axel shook his head. "I only wanted to pay respects to your grandfather. He was a good man."

Samuel sniggered. "You didn't find the labradorite, did you?"

Axel shook his head. "No. I don't think it's there. Maybe he placed it in his room inside?"

Samuel shook his head. "Not there either. If you find it, the stone rightfully belongs to me. I'll need it."

Axel placed a hand to his heart. "I wouldn't dream of keeping it from you. You'll be the first person I tell if I find it."

"Make sure of that," Samuel said.

My heart didn't slow until we were safely inside the truck. "What was that all about?" I said, pulling the ancient black book from my purse and resting it in my lap.

"Samuel thinks the labradorite will give him power that he hasn't had before. Make him a better, more powerful sorcerer."

"Will it?"

"Does putting lipstick on a pig make it pretty?"

I shrugged. "Depends on the pig, I suppose."

He scowled.

"Kidding. No. So you're saying it won't matter for him. He's going to be at the level he's at unless a miracle happens. And some miracles are hard to believe in."

"Right." Axel cranked the engine. "I'm just glad he didn't ask if we'd taken anything else."

"Why not?"

"Because I don't like to lie. At all. Not part of my agenda. And I wouldn't have wanted to give that book up, because I've got a lot of work to do tonight if I'm going to break the connection between you and Rufus."

I placed a hand on his arm. "I appreciate you trying to help."

He turned to me, an almost hurt expression on his face. "There's nothing to appreciate. I care about you, Pepper. I don't want to see anything happen that would jeopardize your safety."

He slid from the parking lot and drove through town. When we passed my street, I frowned. "Where are we going?"

"My place."

My eyebrows shot to peaks. "Your place?"

He laughed. "Don't worry. I'm not trying to seduce you, but I do want to ease that headache. I should be able to, but everything I need is at my house. So that's where we're headed."

I nestled back into the seat and pressed my fingertips into my temples. "Good. Because the sooner the better. This one's getting bad."

He rubbed my shoulder. "Hang on. Just a few minutes longer."

We reached Axel's house shortly after. Unlike all the gingerbread-looking structures in town, Axel's house was constructed of glass and long wooden panels. It looked ultramodern on the outside, and I could attest that it was also ultramodern on the inside with sleek countertops, soft colors and sparse furnishings.

It did not surprise me in the least that Axel rubbed against the grain of Magnolia Cove in terms of the structure. It fit who he was—a man who crashed into oncoming waves in many ways, not just in how he appeared to live.

"I'll try not to keep you here all night," he said.

I pressed my temples. "It's okay. I can stay however long I need to. No one knows I left the house, so Betty won't be waiting up for me."

He quirked a brow.

I elbowed him. "Don't get any ideas."

He guided me inside, where he snapped on a lamp, revealing soft brown leather furniture that looked as slippery as butter. Axel guided me to the couch, and I nestled down onto it. He found a blanket and draped it over me.

"Get comfortable. I'll grab some things and come back."

I rested in the living room while sounds of rummaging wafted from the kitchen and some other room. After a few moments he popped back into view.

"I've got everything I need to calm that ache."

My eyelids fluttered open. Axel sat on the glass coffee table, a wide display of objects scattered atop the surface.

I sat up. A wave of nausea made me pause. "What's all that?"

"This," Axel said proudly, "are the tricks of my trade. A few objects that will ease pain, hopefully diminish it. They won't be able the stem the root of the problem—which is that you must burn off some of your power—but they can at least calm the tidal wave you're experiencing."

"How does it work?"

He grabbed a small cauldron and started dropping items inside—leaves, twigs, fur. He explained as he worked.

"Bark of a willow, a drop of venom from a viper—"

"That's not going to kill me, is it?"

"Shh. I have to concentrate."

I lay back on the pillow. Yep, better let Axel concentrate so that he didn't accidentally kill me, because I did not need to be killed. No, ma'am.

He mortared the mixture, pounding it into a paste. Then he added a few purple drops of liquid from a clear vial. The concoction hissed and wheezed.

He laid a hand atop it, mumbled a few words I couldn't understand. A great puff of smoke erupted from the cauldron.

"It's done."

He poured the contents into a flask and passed it to me. "Snake venom?"

"It's a common ingredient in blood pressure medicine. If it doesn't kill those folks, you'll be fine."

I glared at him.

"Trust me. On this, I know what I'm doing."

"But you're a wizard, not a sorcerer."

He raked strong, muscular fingers through his hair. "I've got advanced training. Drink it. It will help."

I sniffed. "Whoa. That smells horrible."

It did. It smelled like mildewed socks and sweaty armpits. "Do I really have to?"

"Will you stop being such a baby?"

I pushed up on my elbow. "I'm not being a baby."

"Yes, you are."

"But it smells."

"Baby."

Our eyes locked and we both burst into laughter. I sat up and cradled the cup in my palms. "This better not kill me."

Axel brushed a strand of hair from my cheek. "If anything, it'll put hair on your chest before it kills you."

"Very funny... Can I put jelly beans in it?"

Which happened to be my favorite method of sweetening dishes.

He rolled his eyes. "No. The sugar will ruin the perfect blend. Just drink."

So I did what I used to do as a child. I pinched my nose between two fingers and downed the contents.

I nearly choked on the rancid stuff, but I managed to get it gone. I sank back onto the couch, swallowing the bitter aftertaste.

Axel placed a hand to my forehead. "It should work quickly."

The pressure and pain throbbing behind my eyes eased within moments. I inhaled deeply and with each exhale the pain retreated.

"Wow. I feel better already."

I opened my eyes to see Axel sitting in the same spot, a glass of ice water resting beside him.

He offered it to me. "Here."

I took the drink and gulped down several mouthfuls until the last of my headache had vanished.

I plopped back on the cushions and shot him a feeble smile. "Boy, am I sure glad you're back."

"Only because I can cure your aches and pains? You should see what I can do for arthritis."

I laughed. Our eyes locked again, and I felt the tension build between us. It was like a summer storm—thick with haze and humidity, rising and clotting until lightning ripped through the air.

He took my hand and kissed the inside of my palm. I ignored the hormones streaking to my core and instead focused on the work at hand.

"Betty said there were three witches who created the spell that kept Rufus from entering. We spoke to one of them—Sylvia something."

"Spirits," he answered. "Owns the hat shop."

"Right. Who was the other one?"

"Barnaby Battle," he said after tracing his lips over my skin. I had the feeling he wasn't going to be concentrating on Rufus the way I was.

"How do you know all this?"

"I know because I know."

"Cryptic," I chimed.

He sighed, dropped my hand and moved to sit next to me. "I know because there's certain information in town I'm privy to."

"Because?"

He pointed to the cauldron. "Because of things I can do. Spells I can work."

"Because you're super cool," I said.

He chuckled. "Hardly. But those were the three who created that particular blend of magic. So Battle needs to be interviewed. I'm on it. And I've also got to figure out how to break your spell. Battle may have an idea for that, too. He's not a sorcerer, but he's powerful."

"Okay," I said, kneading my fingers into my shoulder.

"You need a shoulder rub?"

I gulped. "Why do you ask?"

He smirked. "You're rubbing and sometimes the tension from a headache will cause muscles to knot in other areas. Like the shoulders and neck. I've got a magical touch."

I have no doubt.

"Sure," I said, feeling daring.

I turned my back to him and moaned as he gently pressed and eased away the knots I could feel lining my neck. "That is like heaven," I said.

"Anything I can do to help," he said. "Why don't you lay on your stomach?"

I quirked a brow at him. "Don't you think that's dangerous?"

He chuckled. "No, I don't. You need to relax."

So I did. I eased onto the couch and let Axel work my muscles until they were butter. I didn't realize I'd fallen asleep until I awoke the next morning.

Sunlight winked through the blinds. I was still on my stomach, and a line of drool ran from my mouth onto the pillow beneath my head.

I bolted up. "Holy crap. My rear end is going to be in a sling and Betty's going to shoot me straight to the moon."

Axel padded into the living room wearing boxer shorts and nothing else. I'd seen him naked in the moonlight once before, but no, I'd never seen his man chest in the light of day.

Oh. My. God.

Little tuffs of black hair sprinkled the top of his pecs, but for the most part he was hairless, and the six-pack that was his abs, I swear I could've bounced up and down on them. I yearned to press my palm against his solid form and stand there for like, ever, feeling the heat wafting off him and salivating at the sheer hotness of him.

Because hallelujah and praise Jesus, Axel was hot.

He handed me a cup of coffee. I took a quick sip and laid it down. "I'd love to stay, but Betty's going to kill me. I've got to get to the store, open up, feed the animals, all that stuff."

In full panic mode, I raced across the room and snatched my purse from a chair.

"I've already talked to Betty."

"Do you want me dead?"

He chuckled and pulled his freshly washed hair into a tight tail. "I explained what happened and that you fell asleep. She agreed to work the shop for you today. And," he said, pressing the coffee back into my hand, "I need you here to figure out that spell. I can't break it if you're not around."

I exhaled. "Okay." I grimaced, still not sure I one hundred percent believed Betty was all right with the situation. "Are you sure Betty's fine with this?"

He smiled. The dimple in his cheek popped. "Cross my heart. Come on. I'll make you some breakfast, and we'll get to work."

I tugged at my shirt. "What about clothes? A shower?"

"We'll stop by the house and get you some. We'll be swinging by there anyway on our way to our first stop."

"Oh? Where's that?"

Axel tapped his fingers against his hips. "To visit Barnaby Battle and find out exactly what went wrong with the spell that's meant to keep Rufus out."

ELEVEN

I decided to shower at Betty's house. So after a meal of a perfect Southwestern omelet, because a Southern one would include barbecue pork, biscuits and gravy—things that were awesome on their own but not so awesome in eggs—we headed over to the house.

Amelia's eyes widened to saucers when she laid eyes on Axel. "Well good morning," she said.

Betty stopped sweeping the hearth. She crossed to me and pressed the back of her hand to my forehead. "Spell's still there."

Axel's cheeks reddened. "I haven't had a chance to work on it, though I was able to calm the headache."

"Good thing." Her eyes washed over me. "Hopefully it won't take too long to get this thing solved. Town's already found out about Rufus. There's a little bit of an uproar about it."

"No surprise there," Cordelia said. "The one man who's supposed to stay out is sitting in jail."

Amelia pressed her fingers to her cheeks. "What if someone breaks him out? Like in a Western. What if then he hides in a cave in town, steals money and does bad things?"

Everyone was quiet. Cordelia snapped the newspaper she was reading. "Your imagination's running away again."

Amelia crunched on a slice of bacon. "Can't help it. It's what I do." She glanced at her watch. "Oh, I'd better hurry. I don't want to be late for my job interview."

My jaw dropped. "At the Vault?"

Amelia straightened the hem of her skirt. "That's right. Betty got me in overnight. Worked some kind of magic. Everyone wish me luck."

We all wished her luck and Amelia left. I went upstairs to shower and dress. While I was slipping into a pair of lightweight pants and a sleeveless T-shirt, I noticed Hugo.

I pulled him from his cage. The dragon curled up on my shoulders. "Looks like you're coming with me today, boy."

I padded back downstairs and found Axel and Betty in deep conversation. They parted quickly when they saw me.

"You ready?" I said.

Axel rose. "He coming with us?"

"Is it okay?"

Axel nodded. "It's great. We might need him."

"You think?"

He placed a hand to my back. "You never know."

We hopped in his Mustang and headed up a hill to a house overlooking the town.

"Is this Battle's house?" I said.

"You got it."

We parked and climbed out. The front yard was fenced, so I put Hugo down and let him play in the clover that dotted the grounds.

Axel knocked on the door. It swung wide, and there stood a tall man with a gleaming smile, a shock of white hair and a tan so deep it looked like he sprayed it on every morning.

The men shook hands. "Axel Reign. Good to see you. I hear we've got a bit of a situation in town. Come on in."

The home was older, with tall ceilings and simple cloth furniture.

The tables and chairs were dark oak and mahogany, clearly antiques. The living room smelled of Old English, suggesting that Battle took good care of his belongings. Or at least someone did.

We sat in the living room, and a young blonde woman entered. "Daddy, can I get you anything?"

It was Delilah, the nurse from the First Witch Center.

"Delilah, come in and meet Axel Reign, if you haven't before."

Delilah nodded at Axel. "I know him from the home." She turned her pretty brown eyes on me. "And you're Pepper, Betty Craple's granddaughter. Nice to officially meet you, though I know I saw you last night, right before Mr. Amulet's body was found." She shuddered. "Horrible. He was such a wonderful man."

I nudged Axel. "Delilah saw Argus not long before he died."

She nodded. "At least, it didn't seem like that long. But then before I knew it, he was dead. Killed himself." Her gaze drifted to her father. "But I see y'all have business to discuss. Can I bring some tea? Coffee?"

Barnaby extended his hand toward a room with large pocket doors. "That'll be fine."

The doors rumbled as Barnaby slid them apart. Once we were inside, he closed them tight and pointed to a couple of horsehair chairs. I sat straight backed, waiting for Axel to talk.

Looked like Barnaby didn't want to wait. "You're here because of Rufus."

"Among other things," Axel said darkly.

Barnaby slid his fingers over his eyebrows. "Let's start there. Y'all are here because a spell that I helped construct failed in some way."

"According to Sylvia Spirits, it didn't fail," Axel said.

Barnaby thumbed his large belt buckle. "But surely it must have for Rufus to have entered."

I cleared my throat. "Excuse me, but I was with Sylvia when she took a look at an image of the spell. To her, every piece seemed to be in place."

"You'll excuse me if I'll disagree with you."

"No need to be excused," I said.

Barnaby stared at me.

"What I mean is that I don't take any offense to you disagreeing at all. Disagreement is a healthy thing. I mean, if we all got along all the time, the world would be, wow, so boring. Don't you think?"

He stared blankly at me.

"Sorry, I talk a lot when I get nervous."

"No need to apologize, my dear."

A rap came from the door. Barnaby slid one side open, and Delilah entered carrying a tray of coffee and tea. She settled the tray on the table.

"Is there anything else I can get y'all?"

"No, that'll be fine," Barnaby said.

She exited and Barnaby started serving. "Poor girl's a mess since the whole thing with Argus happened. Who can blame her? They were close, those two. So close. Sugar in your coffee?"

"Yes, please," I said.

I took the cup and sipped. Axel raised his hand, passing on the refreshments.

"But from what you're telling me," Barnaby said, "it seems as if the spell was either undermined to the point that Sylvia couldn't tell that it had been tampered with or Rufus found a way around it."

"How?" I said.

"He would've slipped through," Axel said, "not disturbing it."

"I don't understand."

Barnaby sat on the couch. "Think of the spell as intersecting lines, sort of like a very dense, very thick web. Under any normal circumstances, Rufus wouldn't be able to slip through, but if he found a way to bend those threads, those fibers just enough that something could pass, then Rufus could slip into Magnolia Cove."

"And that's what you think happened," I said.

"Either that or Sylvia lied," Axel said.

Barnaby shook his head. "I have no reason to think she would work with Rufus. None of us would. That's why we were each picked —we uphold the law and believe in Magnolia Cove. We don't support the sort of magic that Rufus Mayes practices. So, where does that leave us?"

Axel flicked dirt out from under his nails. "It leaves us with the fact that once Rufus is gone, we have to change the spell again, hopefully to one he won't be able to break."

Barnaby snickered. "We didn't think he could overcome that one."

"Magic is fluid," Axel said. "Ever changing."

"Which brings you to your next point," Barnaby said.

Axel lowered his voice. "I think Argus Amulet was murdered."

Barnaby exhaled a deeply. He smoothed his eyebrows again with his thumb. "Proof?"

"I was hoping you could help me with that."

"What do you need?"

Axel pulled the vial labeled DEADLY NIGHTSHADE from his pocket. "I need skunk root. Do you have any?"

Barnaby nodded. He crossed to what looked like a cigar box and opened it. The shiny lacquered wood reflected the sunlight and made the wood appear to ripple like water.

He plucked a vial from the velvet lining and handed it to Axel. "A pinch?"

Axel nodded.

Barnaby uncorked the bottle and poured a small amount in his palm. He then pinched a tiny amount between his forefinger and thumb. Axel opened the vial, and Barnaby dropped it in.

"What are you doing?" I said.

Black smoke blew from the top. It poured from the lip, slipping down the sides like a dark, rolling fog. Something about it gave me the willies. I shivered.

"I'm checking to see if this is really nightshade," Axel said, studying the reaction.

"But you said last night that it was."

He shook his head. "This isn't that vial. This is the one the police had."

My jaw dropped. "How did you get it?"

His cheek twitched. "I didn't. Betty did. Nabbed it from Garrick before he ever even made it out of the First Witch Center."

"She's got some stones, that's for sure," Barnaby said, chuckling. "Leave it to Betty to steal evidence right out from under the nose of the police."

I folded my arms. "So she didn't buy that Argus was a suicide, either."

"There's not much Betty Craple buys," Barnaby said.

"Ain't that the truth," I said. "Okay, so the vial leaking black mist that's almost as thick as blood is the original vial that Argus injected himself with. What have you learned?"

Axel studied me. His lips ticked up into a smile that sent a wave of tingling nerves crashing through me.

I bit down on my lips, trying not to let the smile that wanted to tease out do so. Why? I don't know. I guess I wanted to focus on the task at hand.

"I've learned," Axel said, still locking gazes with me, "that when nightshade reacts with skunk root, it creates a reaction. Skunk root is a reagent and is used to test other potions. It can tell you if something is deadly, or if a potion is fit to be drunk, simply by its color. But when skunk root reacts with nightshade, it creates a very simple yet lovely teal-colored reaction."

"That's black," I said.

Axel nodded. "So it's not nightshade."

"What is it?"

Barnaby snapped the cigar box closed. "Skunk root reacts with two liquids that give off black mist. I know, because I've studied the chemistry of the substance for years. The first reaction is when skunk root is mixed with water. Something about the way the carbons attach causes it to give off ebony vapors."

"That's not water," I said.

"No, it isn't," Axel said. "The second reaction that Barnaby is referring to is a very well-known but uncommon substance. Hard to get ahold of, but can be made with the right ingredients."

"What is it?" I said.

"Strychnine," Axel said. "And there's no way Argus voluntarily injected himself with poison."

"No," Barnaby said. "Argus Amulet was murdered, and this reaction proves it."

TWELVE

*A*xel corked the vial and tucked it in his pocket. "I'll take this to Garrick, let him know what he's really up against."

Barnaby traced a finger over a glossy mahogany desk. "I'll get together with Sylvia and Betty, see if we can figure out how Rufus slipped in."

"Thank you," I said.

He smiled. "Don't thank me. There's a reason we've kept that young man out of this town. The only question, though, is whether or not he had something to do with Argus's murder."

Anger flashed in Axel's eyes. "I'm going to let Garrick decipher that. I'm more concerned with the spell he cast on Pepper."

Barnaby nodded. "Let me know if there's any way I can help."

"Will do," Axel said.

The two men shook hands and we left. I waved to Delilah as we approached the front door.

Axel stopped, his hand on the lip of the door. "Delilah, did you see anything strange that night? Anything at all?"

She pressed her lips as her eyes danced back and forth. "I just really don't remember seeing anything odd. Nothing out of the norm."

"If you do remember, let your dad know. He'll get in touch with me."

She smiled. "Will do."

I collected Hugo from the yard, where he was busy running after a butterfly, and we got back in Axel's car.

"How could Rufus not have been involved with Argus's murder?" I said. "It all makes so much sense. I mean, that's the first thing I thought, too."

Axel turned the key, and the engine roared to life. "I don't know, but I'm going to give this to Garrick, let him work on it." He tipped his head and gave me a dark, intense glance. "I've got other things to worry about."

Meaning me, I assumed. "Okay."

We arrived at the station about five minutes later. Axel slid into a spot. "You want to come in or stay here?"

"I'll come. I'm not going to let Rufus get to me."

I wrapped Hugo around my neck, and we stepped inside. Axel aimed us straight toward Garrick's office. He greeted a few officers as he walked. I noticed that they kept a wide berth. My guess was that they didn't want him to blow their desks away as he'd done to the doors the night before.

Brought the dragon, did you?

I stopped. A cold streak of ice shot up my spine. I slowly turned to the line of cells in back. There stood Rufus, grinning at me.

Wondering if that was me in your head? Well wonder no farther—yes.

I stared at him, and instead of being afraid, I was simply angry. So I marched over to his cell and pointed my finger at his chest.

He sneered like he owned the joint or something. "Listen here, you get out of my head or I will personally let my little dragon give you a sunburn." I patted Hugo. "And I don't think you'd like the way he'd go about doing that."

Rufus raised his palms in surrender. "Understood."

"Good," I said. I turned to find Axel glaring at Rufus. "Come on. Let's go find Garrick."

A few minutes later we sat in his office. A massive scowl marred Garrick's face. He sank his head into his palms and sighed.

"And you're telling me that you somehow got hold of evidence. Evidence that I realized was missing a little after we left the crime scene?"

"I received it from a source," Axel said.

Garrick leaned back. The swivel chair creaked as he stretched his long legs onto his desk. "And I'm guessing that person would've been Betty Craple."

"I don't reveal sources, Garrick."

The sheriff sighed. "I get it." He glanced at the vial, turning it this way and that. "Strychnine, huh? Doesn't sound like the type of poison one of our people would use."

"So it's not the best of the best who did it," Axel said.

Garrick folded his arms. "That's something to consider. I appreciate you bringing this by." He dropped his legs and sat up. "So now I've got one Rufus Mayes jailed, a murder investigation on my hands and a contaminated crime scene. Thanks for making my job harder than it needs to be."

Axel smiled. "That's what friends are for."

Garrick nodded, touching the brim of his hat. "If y'all will excuse me, it looks like I've got a mountain of work to do."

Axel slapped his thighs and rose. "Let me know if I can be of any help."

Garrick frowned. "Like it or not, you already have been."

We left the office. I walked in front of Axel, feeling his protective palm on my back as well as the searing gaze of Rufus as we exited the station.

"Where to now?" I said, shifting Hugo so that I cradled him in my arms.

"My place. I've got to work on breaking the spell on you."

I watched as Magnolia Cove whizzed past. Residents zipped through the air on cast-iron skillets and worked spells on the street. It was a life I never imagined having—not because I wasn't worthy, but simply because I hadn't known it existed.

It was marvelous.

Yet at the same time it was a nightmare. Being subject to a sorcerer's spell without any control or say in the matter was terrifying. I felt weak, unable to do anything.

And that was the real problem here—I could barely work my magic and here I was, vulnerable to someone like Rufus, who I imagined would suck every drop of power from my cells if he could.

But how would he use it?

I suppose that didn't matter. What mattered was stopping him dead in his tracks.

We reached Axel's and I pulled out my phone. "I want to call Betty. Make sure everything's going okay at the store."

He tossed his keys on a side table. "No problem. When you're done, I'll be in the cellar."

"*Cellar?*"

He cocked his head. "Even though you made it sound scary, trust me, it's not. It's just a basement with a dirt floor... Maybe it's got some magical instruments, but for the most part it's a completely normal room."

I tipped my head in a way that said I didn't believe him. He chuckled. "If you're worried, I'll hold your hand the whole time you're down there."

"I'm not a scaredy cat."

He shrugged. "That's where I'll be, and I'll need you to join me."

"I'll be along."

He opened a hallway door and slipped down the stairs. The steps creaked as he descended. I might rethink his offer to hold my hand. If the cellar looked as creepy as it sounded, I would be terrified, y'all.

Betty answered the phone on the first ring. "Familiar Place, where we make all your animal dreams come true. How can I help you?"

"Okay, first of all, we don't make animal dreams come true. That sounds weird."

She scoffed. "Well, what in tarnation would you like me to say? We'll mate you to an animal?"

"No," I said quickly, "that sounds bad. Very bad. In ways I don't

77

want to think about. Just say *Familiar Place* and leave it at that. Anyway," I exhaled, "how's it going?"

"Great. I've already sold a pair of goldfish to a frat boy who promised not to eat them at his fraternity social party."

"Sounds like you've got things under control." *I think.* "You've got my cell number if you need me, right?"

The sound muffled and then Betty came back on. "I've got it. I'll call if I need anything. But Pepper, don't worry about the store. I've got this under control. We will be here. You do what you need to do and trust Axel. He cares about you. A lot."

"Thanks… And do the rest of us a favor and don't steal evidence from any more crime scenes."

"Those cops didn't even know it was evidence. They thought it was a suicide. If it hadn't been for me, they would've thought they were dealing with an open-and-shut case. Open and shut. Like I've said, I run this town."

"As you say."

We hung up, and I dropped the phone in my purse. "Come on, Hugo."

The dragon padded behind me as I moved to the cellar door. I glanced down and saw light illuminating from the bottom of the room. I exhaled a shot of air and took the steps slowly. Every creek seemed to send a slice of angst straight to my heart.

Axel's voice drifted up. "They're not going to break."

"Are you sure?"

"I am."

I reached the bottom and found a dark, cavernous sort of room. The brown dirt floor was packed hard. Clean steel and glass shelving lined the walls, and a white stone worktable ran the length of one wall. The room might've been dug from a hole in the ground, but unless you knew that, it could've existed anywhere, including a world-class laboratory.

I exhaled a low whistle. "This is where you do spells?"

Axel turned around. He was shirtless and wore a black leather pouch around his neck. Strands of black hair had escaped the ponytail holder and framed his face.

I swallowed under his burning stare.

"Welcome to my workroom. This is where I practice magic, learn new spells, that sort of thing."

I cocked an eye at him. "So are you a sorcerer or a wizard?"

"Technically a wizard, though I dabble in some things that stretch those boundaries. Sorcerers tend to call on spirits and use them to do their bidding. I don't do that, though I have on occasion needed to ask the other side for help, but not often."

I sat on a black stone bench. "Okay. You're shirtless."

His lips coiled. "Does it bother you?"

Yes. "No. Not at all."

"Good. Because I need to be this way to feel the magic. To harness the power necessary to break what's been cast on you."

"Oh. Okay," I said, glancing away, a bit embarrassed at how freaking awesome Axel looked and how drool was practically dripping from the corner of my mouth.

Axel rested the book he'd swiped from Argus on a stone lectern and opened it. The binding cracked as he pressed the cover to one side.

"What I'm looking for should be near the front if it's here at all," he murmured. "Or at least that's what I think."

He studied the contents for a few minutes while Hugo padded around, sniffing every nook and cranny of the room.

"There it is," Axel said.

"You found it?" I said, straightening my back in anticipation. "Already?"

He tapped his forefinger against the page. "Looks like it."

"But if Argus had the answer at the very beginning of his book, why did he tell us to give him a day and a half?"

Axel shook his head. "It's not a counterspell that I found. It's an entirely different spell that I think can be worked the way I need it to be."

"What kind of spell?"

"How to remove a spirit that's been sent to attack a person."

I cracked my knuckles. "And this is related?"

"It's close enough. A few tweaks and I think we'll have our solution."

"You're not going to blow us up, are you?"

"Would it be a problem if I did?"

I laughed. "Yes."

"Then I'll do my best not to." He pulled his hair from the ponytail and retied it. "Okay. For this I need you to take off your clothes."

I fell from the bench and landed on my knees. "Ouch! What?"

Red dotted his cheeks. "You have to be naked. Don't worry; I'll keep my back turned while you're undressing."

"This just doesn't sound right."

"Would it make you feel better if I'm nude as well?"

"Yes. No." I grimaced. "I don't know. Maybe?"

"Sorcerer's spells are always performed on those in the nude. That's how it goes."

"Can we turn the lights off?"

"I can work with one candle. But Pepper, I'll have to see a little."

I shoved a hand on one hip. "Why? You need to sprinkle me with pixie dust?"

"How'd you guess?"

"Seriously?"

"Not pixie dust but close. Yes, I have to put magical items on you, and yes, you have to be naked. And before you ask, I can't close my eyes because I have to see."

"You think of everything, don't you?"

He smirked. "Do you want to do this?"

I sighed. "Yes."

"Then I'll turn my back while you take off your clothes. I promise not to look."

He turned around and I started shucking items. "This is really embarrassing."

With his back to me, Axel unbuckled and dropped his pants. My eyes widened. "I don't like being naked in front of you any more than you do."

I rolled my eyes. "Right. You're a guy. And I mean, look at you. You're like a Greek god or something. I'm just normal."

Axel turned his head slightly over his shoulder. "Pepper, there's nothing normal about you. Especially what you do to me."

I swallowed a knot in my throat. "You're not talking about physically, are you?"

He shook his head. "Would you get your mind out of the gutter? No. I'm talking about emotions. Feelings. Guys have them, too. Okay. You done?"

I crossed my arms over my chest, figuring I'd rather he not see me topless. "I am."

For what it's worth, when Axel turned around, he kept his eyes on the book. He blew out several candles until there was only enough glowing so that he could see. He gathered a few items, crossed to me and started chanting.

One of the flames immediately rose. Magic buzzed in the air. The room hummed as if a living force was breathing into it. I closed my eyes, figuring if Axel did look at my naked body, at least I didn't have to know about it.

Sounded like a solid plan.

As the power in the room grew, I could feel the tether tying me to Rufus. It tugged in my head and down my chest. Whatever Axel was doing, it seemed like he'd found the right spell.

The tie between me and Rufus tightened. It felt like someone was squeezing my heart. I had the sense that if Axel pulled hard enough, the connection would snap and I would be free.

That hope made me want to watch Axel. I opened my eyes and gasped.

His arms were covered in fur. So were his legs. The werewolf that resided in him was erupting. His face started to change, elongating.

Fear gurgled in me.

Axel stopped. He exhaled, panting. The fur started subsiding, easing back into his flesh. He threw me a quick look, nodded and started again.

He only got a few words in when the change began anew. He stopped once more, his jaw clenching. Axel tightened one hand into a fist and brought it down on the lectern.

He snapped his fingers, and my clothes flew onto my body, covering me. However he remained naked.

The lights flared on and Axel scowled.

"What is it?" I said.

He shook his head. "I can't work the spell. It's no use."

"Why not?"

His head dropped to his chest. When he gazed back up at me, the scowl on his face nearly sent me running for the door.

"Because Rufus placed a spell over what he cast on you. If I try to break it, I'll change into a werewolf."

I reached for him. "Oh no."

"What's worse—I don't know how long I'll stay in that form." His ocean-blue eyes turned turbulent, like a stormy sea. "I'm sorry, Pepper, but I can't help you."

THIRTEEN

"*L*ike ever? You won't be able to help me forever, or just this once?"

I was grasping at straws made of silly string, hoping that I'd heard Axel wrong. Maybe all he needed was a break, some time to think and he'd come up with a solution for how to break the spell.

He grabbed his jeans and shrugged them on. "I wish I could help. You don't know how badly I want to do that, but Rufus has outsmarted us. If I free you, I change and I don't how long I'll be stuck in my werewolf form. Until the next full moon? Twenty-four hours? How much damage will be done by the time I shift back?"

I gnawed the inside of my mouth for a moment. "Maybe not much. Maybe you'll run to the woods, find a nice place to hole up and return refreshed like you had a vacation."

He pressed the heels of his hands into his eyes. "I wish it was that simple."

I sighed. "Sorry. I know this is heavy. I'm just trying to lighten things up. I don't like being tied to Rufus any more than you dislike that you can't help me."

"That was a complicated sentence."

I clicked my tongue. "I'm a complicated girl." I sank onto the ebony bench. "Do you think there are any other spells in the book that could help? Something to guide us in the general direction?"

As Axel flipped through the pages, something fell from the book and clanged to the floor. Hugo bounded over and sniffed.

I rose. "What's that?"

"A key with a tag."

"A tag?"

Axel nodded. He scooped it up and read the slip of paper. "Labradorite."

"That's what it says?"

He glanced back at the book. "That's it. There's nothing else here." He rocked back on his heels. "Of course."

"What is it?"

He palmed the key. "This key obviously opens some sort of box with the labradorite in it. That stone may be the key to freeing you."

I quirked a brow. "How?"

"If I have the stone and conduct my power through it when I cast the spell, it's likely that I won't change into the wolf. I'll stay exactly like I am."

I clapped my hands. "Great. So. Where does that key lead?"

Axel squeezed it in his palm. "That's a question we need answered, and there's one person in town who knows just about everything."

I smiled. "Luckily we're intimately acquainted with her—Betty Craple."

We reached Familiar Place a few minutes later. Betty was alone when we entered, and she eyed me up and down as if trying to decipher if I'd been kissing Axel, which I hadn't given the incredibly stressful situation. Seeming satisfied with her assessment, she pulled her corncob pipe from the pocket of her floral muumuu and gnashed it between her teeth.

"The spell's not broken," she stated.

"No," Axel said, "but we found a key. I'm wondering if you know where it leads."

"What? Do I look like the Smithsonian or something? I might know a lot, but I'm not sure I can pinpoint where a key goes."

I folded my arms. "Don't you run this town?"

She scowled. "Very funny, using my own words against me."

"I'm a funny gal." I sighed and slumped onto the stool behind the counter. "Rufus placed some sort of counterspell on whatever he cursed me with. If Axel frees me, he turns into a werewolf."

Betty snickered. "Gotta hand it to old Rufus; he's no idiot." She lit the pipe and watched as a smoke ring drifted into the air.

"I'm pretty sure Uncle Donovan wanted this store to be smoke-free."

Betty blew another ring. "What makes you say that?"

"The sign by the door."

Betty's eyes swiveled to the NO SMOKING sign. "That's for customers."

"Right."

She turned to Axel. "Do you think you're the only person the spell affects? If we found another sorcerer to break it, would you still turn into a werewolf?"

Axel grazed his knuckles along his jawbone. "Hard to say. Is it keyed to any individual who tries to free her? That's my guess. Whoever attempts to free Pepper will be faced with revealing or succumbing to their own weakness. The question is, is someone else's weakness easier to cope with than mine? Not as destructive? That's the question we should be asking."

"Hm," Betty said. "Barnaby might be able to do it. Possibly Samuel, Argus's grandson."

Betty and Axel exchanged a long look. Betty snuffed her pipe out by holding her palm over the bowl. "Or maybe none of them will even have a shot at breaking it."

"Barnaby's a better choice than Samuel, but we need to find the labradorite. I get the feeling if we have that stone, I'll be able to break the spell without changing. The labradorite can overcome the part that Rufus wove in."

"So where is it?" Betty said.

Axel lifted the key. "If we can find the lock this fits, we'll have it."

Betty studied the small silver key. It had silver scrollwork and was lightweight, probably hollow inside.

Betty turned it over. "I've never seen a key like this." She handed it back to Axel. "I can't help you. The best I can do is ask around."

Concern flashed in Axel's eyes. "The problem there is Samuel."

Betty tapped tobacco ash into the trash can. "He finds out we have a key to the labradorite and he'll claim it for himself."

I frowned. "But don't you think he'd let you use it on me? Just once."

Betty wagged a finger at me. "That boy's so selfish he won't do it. Either he receives all the glory or no one does. He gets one whiff of that key and he'll have Garrick Young standing at your doorstep to take it. Once it's out of your sight, you'll never see it again. Worse, Samuel couldn't work that complicated of a spell if it bit him in the butt."

"Sounds painful," I said.

Betty nodded. "Magic like that always is."

I pressed my fingers to my temples. "So where does that leave us? Garrick's now investigating a murder. We've got to solve this and work around him. Not to mention that my headache has returned."

Axel shifted on one hip. "Betty—you, Barnaby and Sylvia need to figure out a way to rework the spell so that once Rufus is out, he won't be able to return. Garrick's on the murder investigation, but there may be clues as to where this key leads back in Argus's shack. As much as I want to stay out of this, I really don't like it when my friends are murdered. It kinda ticks me off."

"So what do you want to do?" I said.

He kissed my forehead. "I'm going back to the shack tonight. Now that we know about the key, we may be able to figure out where the lock is located."

"You're taking me with you, right?"

"I wasn't planning on it." I shot him a hard look. He exhaled. "Okay, I guess I've changed my mind. Pick you up at eight."

"Sounds good."

"And I'll bring something to soothe your headache. Or I'll at least try to."

"Thank you."

He slipped the key back in his pocket. "Try to get some rest. You might need it."

"Why?"

He opened the door. "I get the feeling tonight might be a long one."

"Oh?"

Axel tapped his fingers on the edge of the wood. "We don't know what we're looking for and it might take until morning to find it."

With that, he left, leaving me and Betty alone. She turned to me. "You go on home and do as Axel said. I'll be there in a little while."

"You're not going to burn down this store, are you?"

"I was thinking about it. A nice insurance payout would really pad my pocket."

I laughed and glanced at the kittens and puppies, all of which were meowing and whining that they wanted to be played with.

We haven't seen you in days, the kittens said.

Play with us, the puppies chattered.

I raked my fingers over their fur and then scooped up Hugo. "Come on, let's go home and take a nap."

I was walking down the street when I noticed Axel had entered a store—a shop with a key on the outside.

I ducked back in Familiar Place. "Axel's at some shop with a key on the door."

"Well of course he is," Betty said. "That's the key maker."

"Key maker?"

Betty pulled her pants up to her boob line. "Every magical town has a key maker, Pepper. Most people call them locksmiths, but we call them key makers. It was the second most logical place for him to take that key. The first being me, of course."

I rolled my eyes. "Thanks." I crossed the street and headed over to the shop. The large golden key on the door jangled as I entered. The store was a sight. It was like a tea-cup shop, except keys and small golden boxes lined all the shelves. The keys were made of every material imaginable—precious gemstones, rock, metal, wood even. And the small treasure boxes were the same, made of all sorts of organic material and ornately carved.

The place was stunning.

"Welcome," said an older woman with upswept red and gray hair.

Axel glanced over his shoulder. "Hey."

I took a place next to him at the counter and tapped my fingers on the glass as if wanting to see one of the precious boxes on display.

"What've you found out?"

"Pepper, this is Emma Lock, she's the owner of Key Magic."

"How do you do?" I said.

Emma smiled. She was a stately woman in a suit. There was absolutely very little about her that was magical except for the gold monocle that hung around her neck from a golden chain.

The monocle itself floated left and right, no matter which way she turned, as if listening and anticipating her moves.

"Let me see what you have there," she said.

Axel retrieved the key from his pocket. Emma's monocle flew onto her eye and wedged itself under her brow.

"Ah yes, I remember this key," she said. She leaned over. "I understand your questioning is of a delicate nature, and trust me, Mr. Reign, the work we do here at Key Magic is often very delicate. If I remember correctly, this was a very secret request, from Argus Amulet."

Axel's eyes brightened. "That's correct. It belonged to him. Can you tell me what it opened?"

She sucked on her teeth. "It was the late Mr. Lock who created the particular box, may his soul rest in peace. I remember it was the most brilliant blue and green, as Mr. Amulet requested."

"The colors of labradorite," Axel murmured.

"Exactly! Just like that."

Axel rested a forearm on the counter. "Argus didn't happen to mention where he was going to place the box, did he?"

She shook her head. "No, Mr. Amulet never told us that secret. Our clients' secrets stay with them. And Mr. Lock never would've asked. In my business, Mr. Reign, discretion is something we pride ourselves in. In fact, when Mr. Lock constructed the town vault, he had to keep much of the security of the place to himself. Lots of rumors floated around—trap doors, doors that opened to walls, that sort of thing, but I don't know if any of it's true. I don't have a key that will open the vault, and only those who do know how to maneuver the place."

I whistled. "Very mysterious."

"Quite so," Emma said. "Now, that's all I can help you with here. If there's something else I can do, let me know, but otherwise, I have keys to make, Mr. Reign."

"Thank you for your help," Axel said.

We left the store. My skin prickled from the late summer heat. The sun blazed down. I shielded my eyes as the painful throb in my head flared so hard I thought I might pass out on the concrete. Which would be horrible. Because if y'all know how freaking hot it is in the South during the summer, you'd know that the ground would burn my butt faster than pulling down my pants and mooning the sun directly would.

"I'll give you a ride home," Axel said.

I slid into the Mustang. He fired up the engine.

"Where's the Vault?" I said.

"We'll take the long way to your house and swing by there. Why?"

I shrugged. "No reason. Amelia might get a job there, and the way Emma talked, the place sounds creepy and mysterious."

Axel laughed. "Just wait till you lay eyes on it."

"Why?"

He tipped his head toward mine. "You'll see."

"Cryptic," I said.

He laughed. He rubbed the back of my neck as we drove. I closed my eyes, letting him work at the knotted muscles. "You're tense again. How bad's the headache?"

"Horrible, but your fingers almost make me feel as if it could disappear any moment."

"Here we are."

I blinked my eyes open. We were just on the backside of downtown, on a small side street. A tall willow dipped down over a lawn of freshly clipped grass. A building with a circular arch sat nestled behind the tree. Two lion statues guarded what looked to be a steel fortress.

"Do you think Argus placed the box in the Vault?"

Axel shook his head. "No way. The Vault is for government stuff—it's a highly secure Magnolia Cove treasury of spells and magic. It's not for us regular folks."

"Seems intimidating," I said.

Axel whistled. "You wouldn't believe the security."

"Really? Are there armed guards at night?"

Axel chuckled. "Sweetheart, you're in Magnolia Cove, Alabama, the most magical town south of the Mason Dixon. There aren't any living guards at night."

I quirked a brow. "Oh? Then what's the deal?"

Axel grazed his lips over my cheek. I shivered and met his lips. Letting him drink from me eased the pain in my head, but only for a moment.

"Okay, hot stuff, I don't want to get arrested for indecent exposure in your car."

He sat back and threaded his fingers through his hair. "Right. Security. No. No people guard the Vault at night."

"Then what does?"

"See those two lions?"

"The stone ones?"

Axel nodded. "Anyone tries to enter and they come to life."

I grimaced. "I'm guessing they're dangerous."

His eyes darkened as he studied the statues. "They are. Those two lions will rip any intruder to shreds."

Gulp.

FOURTEEN

"I got it," Amelia announced at dinner that night. "I got the job at the Vault!"

I gave her a high five. "Awesome. Wow. That was fast."

"They must be desperate," Cordelia said.

I kicked her under the table. She glared at me. "What's wrong with you?"

"Nothing," she grumbled.

Amelia rolled her eyes. "Listen, Cordelia, I figured you'd be happy for me. I thought for once your general pessimism would be killed in the face of my super awesome happiness."

A smile tugged at the corner of Cordelia's mouth. "Maybe I'm a teensy bit happy."

"Well so am I," Amelia announced. "I start tomorrow."

"Great," Betty said, scooping out mashed potatoes onto everyone's plates. "You can come back and tell us the Vault's secrets."

Amelia shook her head. "You know I'm not allowed to talk about the Vault. Its security is the most important thing in Magnolia Cove."

"No," I said, "guarding Axel when he's a werewolf is. Or even keeping Rufus out would have been, but that's a bust."

Cordelia sipped her glass of tea. "How's that going?"

I shook my head. "It's not and my headache's back. Maybe Axel can stop it. If it gets really bad, I'm going to have to use my power."

Amelia grimaced. "And what about Rufus, what if he morphs your magic to do whatever he wants? Like break out of jail? Make people disappear into an alternative universe? Or even make you gain twenty pounds in like, two seconds?"

I laughed. "But you are right, isn't she, Betty? If I use my power, Rufus can do whatever he wants with it?"

She shoved a forkful of turnip greens into her mouth. "That's not something I want to think about."

"But it's true. The havoc he could wreak could be devastating."

"It would be better if he was devastatingly handsome," Cordelia said.

"I think he's good-looking in a weird sort of way," Amelia admitted.

The three of us glared at her.

"What? He is. Too bad he's sick and twisted. I mean, I'm not saying I'm attracted to him."

"That's exactly what you're saying," Cordelia threw out.

Amelia forked a glob of mashed potatoes into her mouth. "I think you're taking my words out of context."

Cordelia flashed me and Betty a confused look. "I don't think you even know what that sentence means. I didn't take anything out of context. You said Rufus is hot."

"That's not what she said," Betty added. "She said he's good-looking in a weird sort of way. And I agree—the way demons in movies are attractive."

I laughed. "That description fits perfectly. He is like a bloodsucker." A shot of pain raced up my neck, and I planted my face in my palms. "Which is probably what that crazy guy is going to do with my power if he ever gets ahold of it. He'll turn himself into a vampire for real."

Amelia licked potatoes from her fork. "He does have a fetish for that from what I hear... Speaking of fetishes, Cordelia—"

Cordelia's head snapped up. "I don't like the way you put my name with the word 'fetish.' It's kind of freaky."

Amelia smiled. "I probably don't know what the word really means."

"Don't be sarcastic." She folded her napkin and plopped it on the table. "What is it?"

"I was just wondering how things were going with you and Garrick."

Cordelia shot her a look filled with flying daggers. "It's good. We're good. Going slow. Having a nice time enjoying each other's company. That sort of thing." She glanced at her watch. "In fact, he's supposed to be picking me up in a few minutes."

Betty's eyebrows arched with interest. "Oh? Where are you going?"

"We're leaving Magnolia Cove, going to see a movie—that new one about the superheroes saving the world."

"Sounds like you picked it," I said.

"Hardly." She pulled her long blonde hair from her shoulder and released a handful, letting it cascade down her back. "But I don't mind. I just like talking to him."

I frowned. "Is he going to be able to see a movie? You know Argus Amulet's death is now a murder investigation."

Cordelia bit her lower lip. "I'll ask him if he just wants to ride around."

"So you can neck?" Betty said.

Cordelia rubbed her forehead. "Yes, so we can neck so hard I have hickies all over my skin. Who even uses that term anymore?"

"I do."

"Apparently."

The doorbell rang, and Cordelia hopped up from her chair. "That's him." She kissed Betty on the cheek. "Don't wait up."

"I will."

We started collecting dishes from the table when Cordelia opened the door.

And screamed.

The three of us dropped our plates and ran across the room. Well, not Betty—she sort of waddled at an incredibly quick rate, clipping along like *The Little Engine That Could*.

We reached the door. I expected to see a dead body or a ghost. Heck, I actually expected Rufus to be standing there, a blue orb of magic locked between his hands.

But no.

That's not what I saw. Instead, filling the frame was a young man with short dark hair, golden eyes, a nose that looked to have been broken a few times, which made him look genuine and not as polished as he would have appeared otherwise.

"Zach?" Cordelia said.

Holy shrimp and grits. Zach was Cordelia's ex-boyfriend. He was supposed to be somewhere out in the world studying magical history or something. The last place he was supposed to be was here. Tonight. Minutes before Cordelia's new beau appeared to take her out on a date.

"Zach," Cordelia repeated numbly. "What're you doing? You're supposed to be in Borneo."

Zach shuffled his feet. "I need to talk to you, Cord," he said in a deep Southern drawl. "I've made a mistake. A terrible one."

Cordelia glanced down the street. "Well, couldn't you have figured that out earlier? Why are you here now to tell me this?"

Zach's gaze swept over the rest of us. "Miss Betty, a pleasure to see you. Amelia, always good to witness your smiling face. And I don't believe I know you."

Cordelia pointed a limp hand toward me. "Zach, this is my long-lost first cousin, Pepper Dunn."

"How do you do?" he said.

"Fine, thank you," I said.

He dragged his gaze back to my cousin. "Cordelia, I was wondering if I could have a few minutes alone with you? I won't be long."

Cordelia shot Betty a help-me look. Betty boobed her way between my cousin and Zach.

"Listen, kid, for years you've been stringing my granddaughter along. Years. In the whole time you dated, you only visited Magnolia Cove once." She lifted her finger. "One time in all those lonely days.

One time while Cordelia sat by the fire staring at it longingly, hoping you'd return again."

"Okay," Cordelia said.

But Betty wasn't finished. "Only one time you came, while my granddaughter flipped through wedding magazines, imagining herself on those glossy covers. But the whole time you were investigating early caves with magical carvings, while my granddaughter pined for you like no woman has pined before."

"That's enough," Cordelia said. She steered Betty out of Zach's direct line of sight, hiding her behind Amelia, who could only hide Betty in height, certainly not in width.

"I'm here to make up for all of that," Zach said. "I've been a fool, Cordelia, and I don't care who knows it."

He bent down on one knee and pulled a black box from his pocket. He extended it toward her and popped open the lid.

My cousins and I gasped in unison.

Betty stuck her head out from around Amelia's waist. "What is it? Well, what the heck do you know? The boy's got stones after all."

There, cushioned in the box, lay a princess-cut diamond.

"Cordelia," Zach said, "will you marry me?"

Right then the beaten porch boards creaked. Garrick stepped up and strode over, dipping his hat to us. He took one look at the ring, at Zach and then Cordelia.

"Did I come at a bad time?"

FIFTEEN

"Garrick," Cordelia said, grabbing Zach by the collar and pulling him to his feet, "Zach was just leaving."

Concern flashed in Garrick's eyes. His gaze dragged from Zach to Cordelia. He backed up a few feet and raised his palms. "It looks like y'all have some things to discuss. Cordelia, I'll call you later."

Garrick left the porch, and Cordelia turned to Zach. Her face reddened, and I had the feeling that my cousin's lid was about to pressure cook right off her head.

"Years, Zach. We dated years and not once did you ever bother to visit except for that one time."

Betty grabbed me and Amelia. "Come on, let's give them some privacy."

She ushered us back inside the house and shut the door. I could still hear Cordelia blasting away at Zach and his pathetic attempts to explain himself.

"Too little, too late," Amelia said.

"I'd say," I said. A knock came from the back door. "I'll get it."

I exited to the kitchen and opened the door. Axel stood on the steps. "Ready?"

I clicked my tongue. "You saw what was going on, on the front porch?"

He nodded. "Looked intense, so I came back here." He grazed the back of his fingers across my cheek. "What do you say we get out of here? Find ourselves a sorcerer's shack to break into?"

I laughed. "Sounds like a plan."

I said goodbye to my family and followed Axel to his car. When we got inside, I inhaled deeply, drinking in his scent.

"You okay?" he said, quirking a brow. "Getting congested?"

"No," I said, frowning. "Why?"

"You sniffed like you couldn't get enough air."

Heat rose on my neck. No, I was not about to tell him the truth, that I was smelling him and loving it. "Oh, I'm fine. Just testing my nose. Wanted to make sure it was working okay."

Axel fired up the engine. "Is it?"

"Yep."

We slid onto the road. I sneaked a glance back at Cordelia, who looked like she was still giving Zach what-for and hell's bells. His head hung to his chest, making him appear good and chastened.

If you ask me, the guy deserved it for stringing my cousin along for so many years without attempting to make a commitment.

Except now he was.

I thought about loss for a moment and how Axel had lost Argus, a friend, and not long ago my uncle, who had left me Familiar Place.

"Do you miss my Uncle Donovan?"

Axel's gaze dragged from the road to me. "I do. He loved matching witches and familiars. He was great at it, too. A person could walk in the store, and within minutes they'd have their familiar. He was also a caring, good person. You would've liked him."

I stared out the window, watching the light from the streetlamps pool on the road. "I'm sorry I didn't have a chance to know him... If he hadn't drank that bad cider and died, do you think he would've left me the shop anyway? I mean, reached out and found me, brought me to Magnolia Cove?"

Axel nodded. "Without a doubt." We reached the First Witch

Center. He slid into a spot and killed the engine. "Your uncle knew about you and wanted you here, Pepper. But everyone was forbidden from contacting you; otherwise someone would have."

He cupped my chin in his hand and kissed me. "And I wish I'd known about you sooner, too."

I smiled shyly. "It must be my amazing conversational skills that make you say that."

He chuckled. "It's that and much, much more. You snapped me out of my stupid idea that I couldn't get close to someone because of what I am."

I touched his cheek. "You're not a creature. No matter what anyone says. That's not the sum of who you are."

He smiled. "That's what I mean. For so long that's how I felt. Though there's tension here at the town, it's minimal. I can deal with a few distrustful stares. But the fact that you accepted me and didn't care about all that"—he took my palm and kissed it—"you don't know what that means to me."

I smiled. "I'm guessing it means a lot."

"My heart swells when I see you."

We stared at each other for a moment, and then, feeling the tension begin to head, I cleared my throat. "You ready to go investigate the heck out of one sorcerer's shack?"

He grabbed his keys. "Let's do it."

We reached the shack a few minutes later and crept inside. Axel lit an orb in his hand and threw it up. The ball of light exploded outward, dotting the ceiling like a hundred small orbs of illumination.

"That's cool. Do you do constellations?"

He winked. "You ain't seen nothing yet."

I held back a laugh and glanced around the room. "So. We've done this once before. Where do we start?"

Axel rubbed his chin. "Garrick's had his way with the place, so we're just looking for a clue as to where that box might be hidden. Maybe he wrote it down on a slip of paper, or maybe we'll find a contract of some sort. No clue. We just need to look."

I took the back wall, which held a large cabinet with two wooden doors. I opened them. Something furry fell from a shelf directly onto me.

"Ah," I yelled.

"Are you okay?" Axel said, rushing over.

"I was attacked," I whispered. "Something jumped out at me."

He stared at the floor. "It's a ball of string."

I smirked. "It was very scary."

Axel patted my shoulder. "Keep looking."

I dug through the cabinet, finding nothing but dusty bottles until I reached the very bottom. Sitting under a thick coat of grime was a box.

A silver box with a small lock that looked to be just about the right size for the silver key.

"Axel," I said quickly. "Look what I found."

He came over. "Well, what do we have here?" He slid the box from the shelf. "It's heavy." He took it to a table and laid it down.

I blew the grime off the top and smiled at him expectantly. "Do you think the key will fit?"

He fished it from his pocket and grinned. "Let's see." He was about to put it in and said, "This is what I love about my job. As serious as it all is, it's the challenge of putting the puzzle pieces together that fuels me."

I elbowed his arm. "Would you just see if it fits?"

"At your service."

Axel placed the key to the lock. The silver slipped inside, and I felt hope bubble in my chest. I brought my fingers to my mouth. My eyes widened.

Axel turned the key and—nothing happened.

"It's not the right key," he said.

My hopes crashed to the ground. "I really thought this whole nightmare might be over."

A somber look crossed Axel's face. He rubbed my shoulder as I pressed my temples. "We'll get this solved, Pepper. I promise you, I'll do everything I can to free you from this spell." He pressed his hands to mine. "I will do this. Trust me."

I nodded. "I do. I will."

"Let's search a few more minutes. There may be something else here."

I worked my way through the rest of the shelves, ignoring the headache that still fought to take over my focus. I didn't find anything else that appeared helpful. No papers revealing the secret location and no more boxes that could hold the labradorite that we needed.

"Can't we just order some labradorite online? Or does someone else sell it in town?"

Axel nodded. "We could and they do, but Argus's labradorite will be charged with his power. It'll hold spell memories and have energy that we need, sort of like a charged amplifier. If we bought a new stone, it wouldn't hold the sorcerer's power—and that's what we need."

I nibbled the inside of my lip. "Okay, so if we need an amplifier, what about Sylvia Spirits's hats? Could that work?"

Axel shot me an amused look. "You want me to put on a frilly, pointy hat and see if that helps?"

"Yes."

"Okay. First thing tomorrow morning we'll head over there and I'll get one."

I grinned. "Thank you."

Our gazes locked and Axel smiled at me. I tipped my chin and felt the heat rise between us. He took a step forward, cupped my chin and tilted my head back for our lips to meet.

A scream interrupted the moment.

I jerked back. "What?"

He grabbed my hand and waved a palm over the shack. The orbs of light darkened, and he led me from the room.

"It came from the center," he said.

We followed the light spilling from the building. We reached the glass doors, and Axel threw them open.

We found a nurse holding on to a geriatric patient. The elder woman lay on the floor, her arms hanging limply by her sides.

The nurse glanced up at us. "I don't know what happened. She stumbled from her room and collapsed. I shouldn't have screamed. I'm used to death here."

Axel reached out and glanced at the dead woman's arm. He frowned.

"What is it?" I said.

"From the looks of it, this woman had a little help dying. From the puncture marks, it appears she may have met the same fate as Argus."

I grimaced. "You think she was murdered?"

He nodded. "I do believe so."

SIXTEEN

"Ingrid Gale was her name," Garrick said, hovering over the body.

"I think she was poisoned," Axel said.

Garrick sighed. "I suppose I'm going to have to do toxicology on an old woman, just to make you happy?"

Axel shook his head. "You'll be doing toxicology to make yourself happy. I don't know what's going on here, but take a look, make sure it's not related to Argus's death."

I felt bad for Garrick. Boy, had he had some night. First he shows up when Zach's proposing to Cordelia, and now he had more work on his hands than I'm sure he wanted.

Oh well, that's how it goes some days, I suppose. When it rains, it unleashes a flood that disrupts everything in our lives.

"I'll check into it, Reign," Garrick said.

Axel smiled. "Thanks, Young. I don't think you'll be disappointed."

"Hope not, but I could use one less headache this week."

I shot him a comforting smile before Axel and I left. "What do you think's going on?"

Axel dipped his head toward me, keeping his voice low. "I don't know, but we need to find out."

We had almost reached the car when Samuel Amulet shot out from the darkness.

"You have it; I know you do," he said, running toward Axel. "You've got the stone, and I want it back."

Samuel swung to punch Axel in the face. Axel raised a hand, and Samuel's fist got stuck in the air as if an invisible force was holding it back.

"I don't have the labradorite," Axel said. "Now stand down."

"I don't believe you," Samuel spat. "You've got it."

Axel opened his arms. "Where exactly do you think I'm hiding it?"

Samuel's arm relaxed. "Up your—"

"Don't even go there," Axel warned. "Or you'll know what it is to feel a punch."

Samuel crumpled to the ground. "It's all so close. The power. It's within my grasp."

"Did you know another resident died tonight?" Axel said.

Samuel's eyes flared open. "Who?"

"Ingrid Gale."

Samuel's eyes narrowed. "Ingrid was good friends with my grandfather."

"Do you think she might've known where the stone was?" I shot out.

Samuel blanched. "I don't know. Why would I know?"

"You're the one who wants it so badly," I said. Not true. Obviously we wanted the stone as well.

Samuel staggered back. "I've suddenly got someplace to be. But watch out, Axel. If I find you've got Grandfather's labradorite, I will take you down."

"Go for it," Axel said.

"I will," Samuel said.

"Okay."

"Watch your back," Samuel added.

"I don't have to because I could sense you coming a mile away." Axel tapped his nose. "Werewolf smell."

Samuel ran into the night. I glanced at Axel. "Think he had anything to do with it?"

Axel's face darkened. "It's strange that he was here. Why?"

I shrugged. "No clue, but let's get going."

Axel dropped me off at Betty's. When I reached the porch, Jennie the guard-vine dipped down. I stroked Jennie's bud, which made the plant shiver in what I assumed was pleasure, but I learned a long time ago never to assume, y'all, because usually my assumptions ended up being wrong.

When I opened the door, I was met by Betty, a shotgun strapped over her legs.

"Whoa. I thought that whole deal was over. That you trusted me to come in after ten p.m."

Betty stroked the barrel. "It's not for you. It's in case Zach comes back to bother Cordelia."

My eyebrows shot to peaks. "Did he do anything stupid?"

"If you call showing up and proposing to a girl you kept on the hook for three years without making a move stupid, then yes."

I smirked. "I meant anything else."

Betty shook her head. "That was enough."

"Where is she?"

"Upstairs."

I padded up to her room and knocked softly.

"Come in."

I stepped inside to find Cordelia puffy-eyed, crumpled on her bed. Amelia sat beside her.

"Am I interrupting?"

Cordelia shook her head. "No. Come in."

She reached for me, and I took her hand, sitting on the edge of the bed. I didn't even have to ask what had happened after I left, because Amelia filled me in.

"Zach left a little while ago, but not before turning Cordelia upside down."

Cordelia swiped tear-drenched hair from her eyes. "I had it all worked out. I was fine. Really I was. We'd broken up and I moved on.

Then he shows up and throws me for a loop. Why did he have to do that?"

I squeezed her hand. "I don't know. Maybe he genuinely realized his mistake. Sometimes after we lose something, we realize how much we've taken it for granted."

"And Zach took you for granted a lot," Amelia said.

Cordelia knuckled tears from her lashes. "I know. He did. And he's admitted it. Said he won't do it again and wants to marry me."

I frowned. "To make up for it? Or because he's realized his mistake."

"That's what worries me," Cordelia said. "We haven't been in the same space for ages and he shows up with a ring? Says he made the worst mistake of his life by letting me go. While here I am, stupid me, trying to move on. I *had* moved on."

I ran a hand over her hair. "You need to listen to your heart on this one."

"That's what I said," Amelia added.

Cordelia sniffled. "I know. I thought I had it all worked out. I mean, I'm the one who has her crap together, right?"

"What's that supposed to mean?" Amelia said.

Cordelia sighed. "I'm the levelheaded one."

Amelia scoffed. "I'm levelheaded."

I raised my palms. "Y'all, everyone here is levelheaded and smart. Amelia, what I think Cordelia's trying to say is that she doesn't understand why she's got so much turmoil rolling around in her stomach right now."

"I understand that," Amelia said. "I'm glad I'm not in this situation."

"Thanks," Cordelia said drily.

"You're welcome," Amelia said.

The flame in Cordelia's eyes told me she wanted to punch her cousin, so I grabbed Amelia. "We'll give you some space. Come on, cuz. Let's get some sleep. It's late."

We left Cordelia, who I heard burst into a fresh stream of tears as I shut the door. I said a silent prayer for her and slipped into my room, where I found Mattie and Hugo.

I greeted them both, changed my clothes and slipped under the covers. The headache still pinged at my temples, but now it was spreading to the top of my head. I hoped sleep would dampen it.

I sincerely hoped it would because it didn't look like I had any other options for calming it.

By the time I woke up the headache was still throbbing strong. I showered and padded downstairs for breakfast, where I could grab a cup of coffee. Maybe the caffeine would help.

When I got downstairs, I found Betty taking a skillet of biscuits from the fireplace.

"Try one," she said. "By the look on your face that headache is back and in full force. These might help."

They steamed and Betty waved a hand over them. "Now, then. They won't burn."

I dug in. The dough flaked off, and the biscuit melted on my tongue. I moaned. "Wow. That is heaven in a skillet."

She smiled. "Did it help?"

"Not yet, but I'm hoping it does soon." I sank into a chair. "You seen Cordelia?"

Betty shook her head. "No, but when she gets her butt down here, I'll make her eat six of these. They should help her aching heart and make her realize Zach is a sap that needs to be kicked to the curb."

I cocked my head. "Sometimes decisions aren't as easy as we want them to be."

"Bull. Every decision is easy. Just make up your mind and go."

I laughed. "In the perfect world of Betty Craple."

She nodded. "Exactly right."

Amelia bounded down the stairs. "No breakfast for me, thanks. It's my first day at the Vault. I don't want to have any tummy troubles from nerves. You know how I get nervous and then I'll have to go to the bathroom and I might be there awhile. That would be super embarrassing."

Betty and I exchanged a glance. "Well," I said, "on that thought, I'm out of here. Amelia, good luck today."

"Thanks," she said.

I grabbed my purse and headed outside. The humidity was already at a thousand percent, making the air feel like a hot, nasty blanket. It was going to be a blazing day, but summer would soon be at an end and fall would arrive.

Thank goodness. 'Cause every time I even glanced at a sweater in my closet, I cringed. The idea of putting heavy fabric on made me want to jump in a pool—any pool.

Axel had promised to pick me up early. It was too early for Charming Conical Hats to be open, but there was something else I wanted to do and that was talk to Rufus.

I figured I had at least an hour before Axel picked me up, so I decided to head on over to the station.

Not that talking to Rufus would help, but maybe begging would do some good.

When I opened the door, one of the officers greeted me. "I want to speak to Rufus."

The man dressed in a brown fedora, blue shirt and brown vest stared at me for a moment. "He's not allowed visitors."

I bit down on my lip. "Please. It's important. I'm not going to break him out. I only need to talk to him."

"I want to see her," I heard Rufus call out. "After all, she's the reason I'm here."

The officer glanced around nervously. Other than him, the station was empty, but it was still early. "Five minutes."

"Thank you."

When I reached the row of cells, I saw Rufus reclined in a wing-back chair.

"I see you've got some creature comforts. Must be nice. I have a horrible headache that I can only get rid of by using my magic."

Rufus locked his hands behind his head and smiled. "Sounds like quite the predicament."

"It is. I need to be free of the spell."

He laughed. "That's not going to happen, but I tell you what—" He rose and slinked over to the bars. For the first time since I'd met him, I saw what Amelia was talking about—the almost animallike sexuality that sizzled from him.

I swallowed and retreated a step. "Tell me what?"

"You can get rid of the headache; all you have to do is use your power."

"No."

He shrugged. "You don't even know what it'll do."

"I have a bad feeling."

He grabbed the bars tightly. "A bad feeling doesn't always mean a bad reality. Go on," he said, his voice teasing me.

And then I thought about it. We were practically safe. We stood inside a police station with an officer. What was the worst that could happen? Rufus would escape from the cell? But then the officer would attack, tackle him to the floor and throw him back in jail.

Right?

It could happen like that.

But what if it went terribly wrong? Then I would be to blame for whatever happened next.

I closed my eyes and decided to test it. I let some of the fear I'd been holding back trickle into me. It wasn't hard because there was a lot I was afraid of.

"That's it," I heard Rufus say.

The connection between us flared to life. I felt my magic being sucked from me, distorted into something else.

I opened my eyes to see Rufus standing directly in front of me, the cell behind him.

"No," I screamed.

A flash of light appeared, and Rufus jerked and convulsed, falling to the ground, unconscious.

I turned to see the officer with his hand raised, smoke wafting from his open palm. He glanced at Rufus and then to me. He scowled and I grimaced.

"I think it's time for you to leave," he said.

I sighed. "Sorry."

"Get out," he growled.

He didn't have to tell me twice. I scampered from the building and back into the heat.

A pickup truck I recognized slid into one of the parking spots. Axel got out.

"What're you doing here?" he said.

"Causing trouble."

"I hope that's not true."

I cringed.

Axel rubbed his face. "Oh boy. Rufus is still locked up, I hope."

"Barely."

He rolled his eyes. "Come on. Let's get you out of here before you end up arrested."

"Good idea."

I hopped in the pickup, and we headed over to Sylvia's shop. "It's still early. She won't be open, will she?"

Axel grabbed a Styrofoam cup from the holder and handed it to me. "Coffee for you. I've already put the jelly beans in."

I smiled. "Thank you. That was thoughtful."

"I'm a thoughtful kind of guy."

"So I happily see."

I gave him a shy smile, and he grinned in response. My heart swelled with joy, but then the nasty headache of all headaches dinged behind my eyes.

I exhaled deeply and leaned back in the chair. I pressed my fingers to my eyes and waited until the wave of pain subsided. It did, but the darn thing didn't go away completely. No surprise there. It wouldn't. Not until I was able to really use my power. Even that little bit I had thrown at Rufus hadn't done much to put a dent in the headache from heck.

"You okay?"

I nodded. "Yeah. I'll be fine. Let's just see if Sylvia can help."

We reached Charming Conical Caps. Axel helped me from the truck, and we went inside.

We found Sylvia and Barnaby standing over a cauldron. A map of mist floated over the rim of the bubbling iron monstrosity. Blue light flared from the open mouth of the cauldron, casting Sylvia and Barnaby in sickly light.

Both of them stared at the image, and I had a feeling they were making a discovery that needed total concentration.

We paused in the doorway, waiting for them to finish. After a few moments the light faded. The regular lights flared to life, and Sylvia and Barnaby blinked as whatever trance they had been in broke.

Sylvia threaded her hands through her silky hair. She exhaled and gazed around the room. Her attention settled on us, and she offered a wan smile.

"Everything okay?" Axel said.

Barnaby rocked back from the cauldron. He and Sylvia exchanged worried looks.

I gnawed my bottom lip. "What is it? What could be so bad?"

Barnaby sighed. "You'll find out sooner or later anyway. We cast a spell to watch the last three days of the magic that keeps Rufus at bay."

"I'm afraid to ask what you discovered," Axel said.

Sylvia crossed her arms. "It's not good."

"No," Barnaby said. "It looks like the spell wasn't tampered with at all."

I glanced at Sylvia. "That's what you'd said before."

"Barnaby helped me make sure. Just in case I'd missed something when you and your grandmother had been here. But my initial thoughts were right. The spell wasn't tampered with."

Barnaby rubbed a hand over a face dusted with stubble. "Which means that Rufus Mayes discovered a way to slip through. He's grown more powerful than we ever knew, which means—"

Axel nearly growled when he said, "Which means we need a powerful object to keep him out. We need Argus Amulet's labradorite. Without it, we'll be subject to Rufus."

Barnaby's expression darkened. "And Lord help Magnolia Cove if Rufus Mayes can't be kept out."

SEVENTEEN

$\mathcal{W}$e sat at a table drinking coffee. Sylvia brought out a tray of rolls and set them in the center.

"Orange rolls," she said.

I quirked a brow. "Orange?"

She smiled. "The bakery in town makes them. I'm surprised Betty hasn't introduced these to you."

I picked up one of the pastries. Sugary frosting coated my fingers. I took a small bite and moaned. Sugar and orange melted on my tongue as the roll itself dissolved.

"Wow. That's amazing."

Sylvia smiled. "I always keep some on hand for special visitors."

"How's tracking down the labradorite coming?" Barnaby said.

Axel ignored the orange rolls. His loss, my gain. "It's not. We have a key, but no clue what it fits."

He slapped the silver key on the table.

Sylvia glanced at it. "I'm sorry that I can't be of any help here, either. I've never seen a key like it."

Barnaby swiped a napkin over his mouth. "Hmmm. I knew Argus but not his secrets well enough to help. All I suggest is that you keep looking... Speaking of Argus, there was another death at the First Witch Center."

Sylvia's mouth dropped. "There was?"

"Delilah told me about it. Seems she was on duty—working late because another nurse called in. Looks like a suicide."

"I say it was murder," Axel said. "Probably the same person who killed Argus. At least now we can cross Rufus off the list as a suspect. He was clearly in jail at the time of this murder."

Sylvia sipped her coffee. "You don't think Rufus is related to it at all?"

Axel shook his head. "I don't see how. Unless that Ingrid Gale knew where the labradorite is located, why would anyone want her dead?"

Everyone was silent for a moment.

Barnaby spoke first. "If someone knew that Ingrid was aware of the labradorite and they didn't want her to tell us, that's motive."

"But who?" I said. "Samuel seems the most likely choice, but why would he get rid of people who could potentially tell him where the stone is located? That's all he wants, isn't it?"

"So he says," Axel said. "As soon as he gets it, though, he'll vanish and we'll be back to square one."

"It seems we've all got some searching to do. People to ask more questions of," Barnaby said. "If and when you find the labradorite, bring it to me so that Sylvia, Betty and I can figure out a way to keep Rufus out once and for all."

"That's a plan," Axel said.

We finished the snack and Barnaby left. Sylvia flexed her fingers. "So. Tell me how I can help you."

"I don't know if you can," Axel said, "but I've got my fingers crossed that you're able."

"Sounds intriguing," Sylvia said, "which is right up my alley."

"I'm trying to break the spell that Rufus placed on Pepper. Problem is, Rufus infused it with a counterspell—if I attempt to break it, I shift into my werewolf form."

Sylvia tapped her long nails on the table. "Oh, that is a challenge.

You need to somehow circumvent that spell. Are you hoping that by amplifying your magic, you can work your spell quickly enough that Rufus's counter-curse won't take hold?"

Axel leaned forward. His biceps popped in his T-shirt, nearly making me drool. "That's the hope. I'm wondering if it's possible. Have you ever seen anyone do that?"

Sylvia threaded her fingers through her hair. "I have, but not against a foe equal to Rufus. Though even the best sorcerers can be outwitted. At least that's how I think about things." She poked the air. "Anyone can succumb to a spell, but it takes brains more than it does talent to outsmart another witch, or sorcerer in this case."

Axel licked his lips. Intense fire burned in his eyes. "Okay. So my next question to you is—do you have a hat that can do the job?"

Sylvia's lips curled into a devilish smile. "In fact, I just might."

Sylvia left the table and Axel followed. I grabbed the key to Argus's box and tossed it in my purse with a plan to give it back to Axel.

She led us to a large locked cabinet in the main room. Hats topped it and were hooked to the sides, and through the glass doors I saw a wide-brimmed black fedora. It was constructed of leather and weathered, with a tattered brim. A purple plume stuck straight up from the band that ran around it.

"Whenever people ask, I always tell them this is simply a piece that's been in the family for years. Not for sale. And it's not."

Sylvia pulled a gold key from her dress pocket and inserted it. The lock *snicked* and she opened the doors.

A wave of air rushed outward. It felt like I'd been struck by a strong, lakeside breeze.

"What was that?" I said.

Sylvia tipped her head toward the cabinet. "That was the hat."

"The hat?"

Her lips quirked into a smile. "This piece is old, an heirloom as I said. My great-great-grandfather wore it when he hunted mythical creatures—vampires, ghouls, that sort of thing. When he died, he infused the hat with some of his spirt, and from the blast of air that just hit us, I'd say my grandfather's ticked that I haven't let him out in a while."

I swallowed a knot in my throat. "He has consciousness?"

Sylvia pulled the hat from a velvet stand. "As much as a fedora can muster, which isn't saying a lot."

The hat jerked from her fingers and spun in the air on its own. Sylvia sighed. "Sorry, Grandpapa. I know you're in there. I don't know why I said what I did."

If that was supposed to calm the hat, it sure didn't. The fedora spun around the room in a blur of black.

Axel chuckled. "Looks like you've got some making up to do."

Sylvia raised her hands. "I've got a job for you."

The hat stopped. It hung suspended in the air. The brim folded upward as if the object was listening.

"Yes," Sylvia added. "Your services are needed. We need your power to outwit a mischievous sorcerer."

The hat released its brim and tipped downward. Clearly the thing was listening. Remind me not to talk bad about any objects in front of them. It was kinda freaky. The hat's antics almost made me forget about my headache.

Almost.

"Grandpapa, meet Axel Reign. He needs you to overcome a counterspell that's been cast on him. Will you do it?"

The hat flew over to Axel and stopped about three inches from him. The fedora tipped back and forth as if sizing Axel up. It then circled him, inspecting Axel from top to bottom. When the hat was finished, it moved back a couple of feet and dipped down as if nodding.

Sylvia smiled at Axel. "Grandpapa will let you use him. The only caveat is that whatever spell you need to cast must be done here. He mustn't leave this shop."

Axel nodded. "Understood. I have everything in my truck."

He left to retrieve his gear, and a wave of pain shot from my head down my spine.

"Ah," I said, folding over.

Sylvia grabbed a chair and brought it to me. "Here. Sit. Hopefully this will all be over soon. Let me get you a cold compress."

She rushed off and returned with a washcloth that I draped over my eyes. "The headaches are getting worse. I don't know how much longer I'll be able to take it."

She squeezed my arm. "Maybe Axel will break the curse with my grandfather's help."

"I hope so," I murmured.

I heard Axel enter the room. I pulled the cloth from my eyes and sat up.

"Everything okay?"

I smiled weakly. "Fine. Just a little pain. No big deal."

I watched Axel and Sylvia exchange glances and knew my lie hadn't worked.

"Sylvia, do you have a private room where we can work?"

She motioned for us to follow. "Come to my spell room. Once you close the shades and shut the door, it's nearly pitch-black, perfect for what you need."

Sylvia left us alone with the hat, and I couldn't help but feel like her grandfather was watching me. Part of me didn't want to disrobe in front of it, but the other part of me was in so much pain I couldn't give a rat's behind either way.

"You don't have to take off your clothes," Axel said.

My eyebrows shot up. "Why not?"

"I first want to test it, see if this will work. There's no point in going through all the steps if it won't."

I toed the floor. "So then how're you going to know if it works?"

He smiled. "I'm going to disrobe since I'm the person the spell affects."

"Okay. Great idea."

"But be ready to take everything off if I signal for you to."

"And I thought I was going to get out of being naked in front of you."

"You're not that lucky."

"Or *unlucky*."

He paused. "I'm not sure if that's good or bad."

"Me neither."

He crossed over and wrapped his arms around me. I inhaled his scent and exhaled, letting the tension melt from my shoulders.

"Thank you for trying so hard for me," I said into his chest.

He took me by the shoulders and pressed me away. The look of concern in his eyes made my knees liquefy. "I care for you. How many times do I have to tell you that?"

"I know...I just—"

"Can't get used to a guy who treats you the way you should be treated?"

I smirked. "I wasn't going to say that."

But it was true. My last boyfriend cared more about fantasy football than he did about me.

Loser.

But it had taken me a long time to realize that—to see that I deserved so much more. Of course, he had also broken up with me; it hadn't been the other way around.

In the short, rocky relationship that I'd had with Axel, I understood that I deserved to be cared for by someone who only wanted the best for me and who would move mountains if he had to.

Like how hard Axel was working now.

"Listen," Axel said, "when this is over, I'll take you out of Magnolia Cove. Even if it's only for a day. We'll go and breathe a little. You deserve that."

"Thanks," I said.

"Now. Are you ready?"

I placed a hand over my eyes. "You may strip."

He laughed and I listened to the shuffling of clothing as he did what I'd commanded.

"All right," Axel said, "let's put this hat on and work a little magic. You can open your eyes."

I slid my hand from my face. Axel had the winked lights out while he'd changed. A single candle glowed, illuminating him with the hat pulled down to his eyes.

I had to say, he looked pretty sexy. He'd certainly give any of the current Magnolia Cove police squad a run for their money.

The room buzzed as magic filled the air. Axel raised his arms. The hat itself hummed with energy. Axel spoke the same words he had before. I started to feel the spell binding me to Rufus tighten.

My eyes flared as the line holding me strengthened. "It's making the bond stronger," I said.

Axel's gaze flickered to me. "It's only a reaction to me trying to break it. Hold on, Pepper. Just hang in there."

He went back to the words, and I felt the line start to pull at me so strongly that it seemed my heart might rip right from my chest. I inhaled, hoping the sensation would stop, but it didn't.

Instead, it worsened.

"Axel," I gasped, "I think it's going to kill me if you keep up."

"Almost done."

Wasn't he listening?

"I won't make it," I said.

He stopped. Stared at me. The tether strained, and I knew if Axel said one more word, something would give and that something would be me.

"Stop," I panted. Sweat sprinkled my brow, and I gulped down air, forcing back the pain in my chest.

Axel's arms dropped to his sides in defeat. He nodded and crossed to me, taking me in his arms.

And yes, he was naked, but I tried to ignore it.

"What happened?"

I pulled away from him and slicked my soaked hair from my face. "I don't know. It felt like if you kept talking, it would kill me. It wasn't like before when you worked the spell. I literally thought my heart would burst from my chest."

He grimaced. He took a step back and pressed his fingers to his mouth in thought. "The hat wouldn't have done that. In fact, the hat worked. I didn't feel like I was going to shift at all. But since that didn't happen, there was another lock put into place."

I tilted my head. "Another lock?"

He nodded. "Rufus is smart. *I* didn't change, but you felt like you were going to die—and my guess is that's exactly what would've happened if I'd finished. It would've killed you, but you'd have been free of Rufus."

"Not a better choice."

"Right." Axel pressed the heels of his hands to his eyes. "That jerk. He knew I'd work the spell on you, and that's been his plan the whole time. And he also made sure I won't be able to have any help in overcoming it. If I do, the spell will kill you."

I frowned. "What do you mean?"

When Axel looked at me, the turbulent ocean of his eyes nearly drew me into a crashing wave. "I mean Rufus wants me to turn into the werewolf. His plan all along has been to unleash the beast on Magnolia Cove."

I closed my eyes. "Oh no... What can we do?"

"What choice do we have?" Axel said. "At some point we'll have to release the werewolf."

EIGHTEEN

"*T*he hat won't work," Axel said to Sylvia.

She frowned. "I assume this isn't user error."

He shook his head. "No. It's another counterspell Rufus cast on Pepper's curse."

Sylvia ran a finger over the rim of the ancient fedora. "That Rufus, always ready to make trouble."

"More like always ready to outsmart everyone," I said.

Sylvia gave me a side-eye. "There you are correct."

"The hat did its job," Axel said. "But if I break the spell with it, I'm placing Pepper's life in danger."

"Hmm," she mused. "Not a good option. Your best chance is to find that labradorite. Barnaby has a lot of experience with it and shifters. He might be able to help if you turn. The stone has enough power that it might be able to force a shift back to your human form. Mayor Battle could facilitate it." Sylvia stared at the hat for a long time before her lashes fluttered and she gazed on me. "What I'm about to do has never been done before."

She took the hat and handed it to me. "If you need it, you may use it. I trust that it won't be Axel who needs this hat, but you, as you're the one who's affected by Rufus's spell. Don the hat wisely and amplify your power however you need to."

I smiled weakly. "It's an honor to have such an object."

"It's not forever," she said quickly. "Only a loan."

"I understand."

With that we left Charming Conical Caps. Warmth from Axel's hand spread up my back.

"Sylvia likes you."

I shrugged. "It's just a hat."

He shook his head. "Not just a hat. A powerful talisman."

I held the hatbox in my hands. My fingers trembled as the fedora pulsed with power inside.

I grinned widely. "Well, let's just hope I don't screw it up."

〜

"WE NEED to chain Axel tonight, under the moon," I said to Betty.

Once Axel and I had left Sylvia's, we headed over to Familiar Place to chat with Betty over glasses of sweet tea that we'd picked up at Spellin' Skillet.

I slurped from the Styrofoam. "It has to be tonight."

She shook her cup until the ice clinked inside. "Why?"

"My headaches are getting worse."

Axel nodded. "I don't want Pepper to be in any more danger than she already is."

Betty sat the cup down. "I promised Barnaby and Sylvia I would help them construct the new spell to keep Rufus out."

"I don't need you there. I can chain Axel myself, but I wanted to make sure you knew and approved."

She cocked an eyebrow. "You need a third person. What if something goes wrong?"

To be honest I didn't want a third person there, y'all. The ritual was private, personal. I only wanted it to be me and Axel.

"And what about changing back into you?" Betty said to him.

Axel raked his fingers through his hair. "I'll let that take care of itself."

A wave of panic rushed through me. "Axel, she's right. I don't know why I didn't think about that before, but we don't know when you'll shift. What if you don't?"

Betty adjusted her wig. "She's right. What if you don't?"

Axel sank onto a stool and stretched his legs in front of him. "What if I do? What if the changing spell only lasts five minutes and then it's over?"

"Do you really think Rufus would do that?" Betty said. "Ha! You're more of a sucker than I thought. There's no way in all of creation that Rufus would create a spell specifically for you that would last only a short time."

He slapped his thigh. "What am I supposed to do? Pepper's headaches are getting worse. I'm sure Rufus anticipated that. He knows we have to free her. If she's allowed to use her power with him sucking it away, there's no telling what he'll do. If I don't do something, she will be hurt. I have choices, options. Pepper doesn't."

"And the stone?" Betty said.

"Vanished. I don't know where to find it and no one we've asked has been any help."

Betty hummed to herself. She clasped her hands together and rocked up on her toes and back on her heels. "I think this might be an irresponsible choice."

"It's my choice," Axel said, a low growl emanating from his throat.

"I wasn't finished, young whippersnapper."

"Go on."

"You're caught because a rock and a wall of concrete. I understand, but you're being foolish if you think the spell Rufus cast to change you will only last five minutes. It won't. If Rufus has anything to say about it, you'll be stuck as a werewolf for a long, long time."

Axel folded his arms. "Not if we find the labradorite. That stone has a lot of power. It could be used on me."

"You've said yourself it's gone missing. I don't like it. It stinks of foul play. I think you'd be better off tracking down that stone instead of giving in to what Rufus wants."

I rubbed my temples. "He's smarter than I realized. To have set all this up."

Betty nodded. "The chaos Rufus brings is criminal. He won't get away with it or my name isn't Betty Craple."

Her tenacity made me smile through the pain of my aching head. "But we're trapped. We need the labradorite, but if Samuel discovers we've found it, he'll steal it. What are we supposed to do?"

"I'll reach out to a few friends on the city council, ask if they have any ideas of where to look for it." She glanced at me. "Meanwhile, I suggest you get some rest. It'll ease the headaches."

I glanced around the store. "You sure you don't want me to stay? Help you out?"

She shook her head. "No, no. I'll keep this place going. Don't you worry about that."

Axel dropped me off at the house. "Do you want me to come in?"

I shook my head. "No. I'll be fine. I'll get some rest." I pressed my forehead to the glass. "So everything hinges on the labradorite."

He drummed his fingers on the wheel. "It doesn't have to."

I glanced over at him. "What do you mean?"

He grimaced. "I know it's risky, but we're nearly out of options. Your headaches will increase to the point that you won't be able to bear them anymore and I'll be stuck watching you suffer, knowing the whole time I can fix it. I can make you well."

I rubbed his bicep. "What are you saying?"

Axel gripped the steering wheel until his knuckles whitened. "I'm saying there is a choice. It's not a perfect one, but it's there."

"I don't want you turning into a werewolf without a way of changing you back."

He shook his head. "Don't you see? We might not have a choice. This is what Rufus wants—to make us out of options, out of possibilities, which we are. I'm not putting a whole lot more faith in finding the labradorite. I'm not going to stop looking. After this, I'm heading over to the Vault to ask a contact there if they've seen a match to this key."

"The Vault?"

"Where else could the box be? But like I said, I'm not giving this much more time. I'm not going to watch you suffer, especially when I have the means to help you."

"Axel, I don't want you to sacrifice yourself for me."

"What am I sacrificing? I won't be a wolf forever. Somehow I'll shift back. I'm not worried about it." He smiled tenderly at me. "I'm worried about you, Pepper. *You*. Not me."

I rubbed my forehead. "So what are you saying?"

He turned to me and stroked my cheek. "I'm saying that tonight, labradorite or not, I'm performing the ceremony."

"Axel..."

His expression darkened. "I'll become the werewolf."

NINETEEN

I held my breath. My lungs burned. Finally I exhaled a deep shot of air. "I don't want you to do that. I don't want you to sacrifice anything for me."

He stroked my cheek. "What's life without a little sacrifice?"

"A nice long one."

He chuckled. "It's my choice. Don't worry. Everything will work out. You'll see."

"But Axel—"

"This is my choice," he growled. "You can argue with me as much as you want, but it's not going to change my mind. Period. Now go inside and get some rest. We've got a big night ahead of us."

I pressed the heels of my hands to my eyes. I sniffed and then drew them away. "Okay. I'll accept what you want, but I wish there was another way."

"There still may be. Maybe I'll find the box."

I squeezed his arm. "I hope so."

He kissed me long and deep before I headed into the house. As I marched up the steps, a thought knotted my brain.

Axel may want to save me, he may think changing is the only way to do it, but I won't let him. No way. When he comes and wants to perform the ceremony, I'll resist. That's what I'll do.

It was the best option. The thought of Axel shifting into a werewolf with no idea when he'd change back was awful. Truly horrible. It wasn't something I could deal with, and to be fair, I didn't think Axel deserved to be cursed because of me.

He deserved to live his life the way it was supposed to be, not chained up in the Cobweb Forest until such time as he changed back into his human form.

No. Allowing Axel to become the wolf wasn't going to happen. I cared for him too much.

I hoped he understood when I explained it to him.

I entered the house. Sitting on the couch was Zach.

Cornelia's Zach.

"Pepper, right?" he said.

I nodded. "How're you doing?"

He rubbed his thighs as if trying to get the wrinkles out of his khakis. "Oh, I'm great. Cordelia's in the kitchen whipping up some lunch. Would you care to join us?"

I couldn't hide the grimace that lit my face. "Um. No thanks. I've got some very important work to do that requires my full attention, and I have to do it away from people."

Zach looked at me as if I had two heads.

What can I say? When I get nervous, I talk a lot.

I went into the kitchen to find Cordelia. Mattie and Hugo were in there with her.

"Hey, y'all. What's up?"

"Mama," Hugo said.

"Hey, sugar," Mattie said.

I picked up the dragon, placed him on my shoulders and immediately realized how much worse the added weight made my headache, so I set him back on the floor.

Cordelia was building a couple of sandwiches.

"You putting poison in his?" I said.

AMY BOYLES

She smirked. "Don't tempt me."

I laughed. "What's he doing here?" I whispered.

Cordelia slapped a lettuce rib on his sandwich. When I say rib, that's all it was—not the leaf, just the spiny part. When Cordelia made a statement, she made it bold.

"He said he wanted some time to plead his case, talk things over more."

"I thought he did that last night."

She pulled her hair back into a ponytail. "Should I drop one of these on his ham?" she said, eyeing a strand.

I brushed her hand away. "I think he'll get the point by the lack of lettuce."

She stared at the hair for another moment before releasing it. "I guess you're right. Anyway, he said there was more he needed to say, and stupid me, I promised to listen."

I hugged her. "It's not as easy as you thought it would be."

She knuckled away a couple of fresh tears. "I told myself that if I ever saw him again, it would be easy to walk away, but it hasn't been. Not like I assumed. I mean, if I was Betty, I would've pulled out my shotgun and told him to run." She laughed bitterly. "But I guess that's not me after all."

"Not all of us can be Betty Craple, and Lord, I thank heaven every day that that's the truth of it."

Cordelia laughed again, but this time it was genuine, coming from her gut. "Pepper, what do I do? I'm so confused right now."

I took her hands. "Listen to your heart. If you feel like Zach's being honest and if y'all marry you'll really be joined, then I say go for it. But if you feel like all he'll want once you marry is to run off without you to some cave, it's not worth it. I don't know him, so I can't make this decision for you."

She yanked a tissue from a box and blew her nose generously. "I don't like complications. I like things to be smooth and easy—no ups, no downs."

I hid a smirk. Cordelia always had a quick, sassy word and seemed so put together. This just proved that anyone could be thrown for a loop—especially when it came to matters of the heart.

"You'll figure it out," I said.

"Enough about me," she said. "What's going on with you and this whole stupid Rufus spell thing?"

A sharp jab of pain streaked through my head. I cringed. "Don't you want to take Zach his plate?"

She waved an elegant hand. "Why rush? He made me wait three years. He can sit for a few."

"In that case, not much is going on. Axel's gone looking for a box that supposedly holds the labradorite in it, but even if he doesn't find it, Axel wants to work the spell that will free me even though it will turn him into a werewolf—possibly for good."

Cordelia's jaw slackened. "You're kidding."

"Yes. No. Sort of—to be honest, we don't know how long he'll be stuck in the wolf form, and I don't want to find out. I won't have Axel risking himself for me."

Cordelia placed a warm hand on my arm. "You've got with Axel what I always wanted from Zach—a man who will do anything for you. He's willing to sacrifice himself for the woman he cares about. The only thing Zach was willing to do was call every few days and brag about what discovery he'd made. If once he'd shown me that if there was a mountain between us, he'd chainsaw that sucker down to get to me, things might've turned out differently—but he never did."

She sat quietly for a moment.

"It looks like you may have your answer about him," I said.

She nodded stiffly. "I think you're right." She threw her arms around me. "Cousins are the best—especially long-lost ones."

I held her tightly. "Don't forget—we're the sweet tea witches."

"That we are," she murmured.

I stepped back and smiled. Cordelia would be okay. Zach would be out on his butt, but that's what that guy deserved, in my opinion. Cherish what you have when you have it, not after it's gone.

Tears misted Cordelia's eyes. "Here, let me get you another tissue." I swept my arm over the table and in the process knocked my purse.

Argus's key spilled from the center, tumbling onto the wooden surface. "Crap. I forgot to give that back to Axel."

"What is it?"

"It's the key that goes to a box located somewhere. What it actually is, is a pain in my butt. If Argus had left some sort of clues as to where the stupid box was, life would be so much easier, but he didn't."

The back door opened and Amelia entered. "Whew, is it hot out there or what?"

"It's hot," I said. "That's for sure."

Amelia's gaze settled on the sad-looking sandwich Cordelia had made. "Who's that for?"

"Zach," Cordelia said. "He's in the living room. We're supposed to be having lunch."

Amelia's eyes widened. "He's here?"

"Yeah, he's like a boil that just won't go away, or come to a head."

"Or like one that never should've existed in the first place," Amelia added.

"Yep," I said.

Amelia plopped into a chair at the table and picked up the key. She twirled it between her fingers. "So what're you going to do about Zach?"

"Tell him to get lost," Cordelia said. She glanced at me. "Pepper helped me figure it out. I've already wasted too much time on him. I don't need to waste another second." She rose, smoothed out her clothes and grabbed the sandwiches. "Wish me luck."

"Good luck," I said.

With that, Cordelia disappeared through the swinging door and into the living room.

Amelia stared at the key for a few more seconds.

"I'd pay you a million dollars if you could tell me what it goes to," I said, joking.

She stared at it. "There is something familiar about the design on it."

My eyebrows shot up. "Really?"

"Yeah. There's a box at the Vault that matches it."

I grabbed Amelia by the shoulders. "You're kidding, right?"

"No."

"But how could Argus have a box there? I thought only town secrets and high-level objects were stored there."

"They are, but sometimes if a witch or wizard served in the government in a high-ranking office, they're allowed access to store limited objects."

My eyes flared. "That's right! Argus served during some werewolf war that he mentioned."

"It makes sense. Most of it is pretty top-secret stuff, but some rooms are lower-level security. That's where I saw this same scrollwork."

I grabbed her shoulders. "Oh my gosh, Amelia. You've got to get me in to see it. That may be the box Axel's been searching for."

She dropped the key with a *clank*. "Pepper, I only just got this job. I can't risk it. If I were found to have let you in, I'd be fired, possibly arrested."

I got down on my knees. "Is there a way? Anything you can think of?"

Amelia placed her hands flat on the table. "Security is tight."

"What about the key itself? Will it get me in?"

Amelia gnawed her lower lip for a moment. "Yes, the key will get you into the outer office, but if Argus didn't allow you any clearance, there's no way you'd be able to get farther than that. If he did give you clearance, then you'd be able to go as far as the key would take you— directly to the box."

"Okay," I said quietly. "I know there's no way in high heaven that Argus would've given me any kind of clearance."

From her spot on the floor in a sunbeam, Mattie opened one eye. "You're forgettin', sugar, that Axel and Argus were friends."

I clicked my tongue. "Close enough that Argus would've given Axel access to the box?"

Mattie yawned. "There's only one way to find out."

I nodded. "There sure is."

I fished my phone from my purse and dialed Axel's number. He picked up on the first ring.

"I know where the box is, and I need you to meet me in ten minutes."

TWENTY

*T*en minutes later Amelia and I met Axel in front of the Magnolia Cove Vault. Just looking at the lions guarding the place sent a shiver straight down my spine.

"I'm glad you called," Axel said. "I'd stopped off at my house for a few things and was on my way here."

I nodded toward Amelia. "She says there's a box matching the key's scrollwork inside."

He studied Amelia. "You sure?"

She gestured wildly as she spoke. "Yeah, I think so. I mean, I'm pretty sure. Heck, I've only been on this job for a day; there's still tons of stuff I don't know. Like I told Pepper, the key will get you to the outer chamber. Unless you're on Argus's approved list of people to enter, you won't be allowed access."

Axel nodded. "Which means we'd have to break in."

I stared at the lions. "And be torn apart by those?"

He shrugged. "I can be fast when I need to." He pressed a hand to my back. "Let's hope it doesn't come to that."

"Let's hope," I said weakly.

"So we're on our own?" Axel said to Amelia.

"Yep. New job, new and better pay. I don't want anyone to blame me if you end up breaking in, thank you very much."

"I wouldn't tell anyone you helped us, if that makes you feel better," he said.

She shifted her feet. "Yeah, well, that almost makes me feel better."

Axel stared ahead before glancing down at me. "You ready?"

I swallowed. "Let's go."

We walked the long concrete sidewalk, slowly approaching the building. A willow draped the entrance, and a long shadow fell from the afternoon sun.

I studied the lions. As we neared, their bodies appeared to sparkle as if someone had thrown a handful of glitter on them.

"What are they doing?" I said.

"Coming to life," he said.

I locked my knees. "Are you kidding?"

"No."

I curled my fingers into his shirt. "I thought they only did that at night if you were going to break in."

"Oh, I forgot to tell you—they sniff everybody out before you can enter."

I wrinkled my nose. "Why?"

He shrugged. "No clue. But I've heard if they don't like the way you smell, they eat you."

I stopped right there in the middle on the sidewalk. "You're kidding, right?"

He smiled down at me. "I think so, but like I said, it's a rumor. So I guess we'll find out."

I started to turn back. "I'm not finding out."

He grabbed my arms. "Come on, Cowardly Lion. You can do this."

A jolt of pain raced across my forehead. I paused, taking a deep breath.

Axel pulled me up. "Do you want to go back?"

I stared at the lions, the Vault and Axel. I was not a coward. My time in Magnolia Cove had proved that to me.

"I'm going forward. Let's do this."

Hesitation and panic bubbled in my veins as I approached the animals. Though I'd convinced myself I needed to walk past them, I really didn't want to. All I wanted to do was tuck my tail between my legs. But still, I'd come this far, and I could take a few more steps to secure the prize of Argus's labradorite.

The glittering lions sparkled into flesh. I sucked air, but Axel's reassuring hand on my back gave me an injection of confidence.

"It's going to be fine," he murmured in my ear.

"This is like in that movie *The Neverending Story* when that boy Atreyu, who was really cute when he was a boy but isn't nearly as good-looking as a grown man, had to walk between those two sphinxes and try not to get fried by the laser beams that shot from their eyes."

Axel paused. "Yeah. Just like that."

The lions growled, and I swear saliva dripped from their fangs. They pawed the air. Axel shifted to guard me from them, placing himself in front.

"I thought you weren't afraid of them," I said over his shoulder.

"I'm protecting you."

"I thought we wouldn't get hurt."

He glanced over his shoulder and shot me a scathing look. "Would you just focus?"

"It's okay if you're nervous. I'm nervous too."

He rolled his eyes and returned to leading me between the lions. The one on the right sniffed Axel up and down, peeling back its lips to reveal razor-wire-sharp fangs.

We're almost through, I thought. Just think happy things and we'll be fine. We'll make it without any problems.

I peeked around Axel and saw the lion sniff him and then turn away, as if he wasn't interested anymore. The second lion did the same.

Whew. We were scot-free. I was about to be inside the Vault, having gone through some sort of mythological Greek trial. I swear, throwing me in a maze with a Minotaur and saying I had to find my way out before the creature found and ate me made more sense than being judged by two magical lions.

I'd exhaled a breath that started all the way in my toes when I felt a paw hook into my shirt collar.

"Axel," I squeaked as I released my hold on him.

The lion tugged me back. Hot breath poured down my neck.

Axel whirled around. His eyes flared in fear. That was not good. Oh boy, was it not good. Like, really not good. I just knew it. I felt it in my gut—a gut that was churning, which meant I'd have to make a pit stop in the restroom as soon as we got inside.

Man, I really hated having tummy troubles in public. There was nothing more embarrassing than having to stink up a public restroom. Of course, I always hid in the corner toilet and made sure everyone was gone before I exited so that no one could see who it was creating such a horrible smell.

I'm sure none of y'all do that.

"Stay calm," Axel said.

Fear had frozen me solid. He did not have to worry about staying calm because I certainly wasn't about to start waving my hands in the air like I just didn't care.

A sharp claw scraped down my neck before hooking into the fabric and yanking me back another step.

"I'd face them if I were you," Axel said.

"You're not me."

"Just do it."

I exhaled and slowly pivoted. Two large sets of teeth greeted me. Panic scrambled up my throat and nearly escaped as a series of screams, but I bit it back down and faced the creatures.

The one on my right opened its mouth and roared, creating a wind that whipped up my hair and fluttered my clothes.

Please don't eat me.

The lion glared. I'd always read never to look a creature in the eyes because they think it's confrontational, so I stared down. Finally the beast looked away, uninterested.

I turned to go when the second lion snarled. I stopped and waited as the creature sniffed me over one more time and then settled back into a resting position.

Relieved, but nearly about to pee my pants, I dashed to Axel and grabbed his arm.

He squeezed me tight. "You made it. See? I knew you could do it."

I grimaced. "There's something I need to do as soon as we get inside."

"What's that?"

"Visit the ladies' room."

AFTER A QUICK DETOUR, we stood inside the Vault. The place was a fortress. Glittering black stone lined the walls, making the structure as foreboding as anything I'd ever seen.

"What's it made of?" I whispered to Axel.

"Onyx. Many times onyx can be used to nullify magic. It keeps the Vault safe from being broken into."

"So Danny Ocean and the *Ocean's Eleven* crew can't show up and pull a heist?"

"Just like that."

I clicked my tongue. "That's what I thought."

"Come on," Axel said, grabbing my elbow gently. "We've got to find the guardian and show him the key."

He led me to the back of the main circular room. There, standing before what looked like a prison cell made of onyx, stood a man in a long white robe with a lectern in front of him.

He had dark skin, a white beard and silvery hair that was braided down his back. His face was long and drawn, pinched up as if he was perpetually constipated.

Gosh, I hoped not. That would be horrible. Now I sounded like Betty. Old folks were more obsessed with constipation than any other age group that I'd encountered. And this guy was old—not quite ancient but definitely old.

"How can I help you?" he said without looking up from a book settled before him.

"I have a key."

The man blinked and glanced at Axel. "That's wonderful. A key. Will it get you in?"

Axel's jaw tightened. "I don't know. That's what I'd like to know."

"May I see it?" the man said.

Axel glanced at me. I suddenly remembered that I had it. I opened my purse and started fishing through the contents.

"Now where did I put it?" I dug past used tissues, lipstick, a hairbrush, feminine products, gum, pens, pencils. "Nope, it's not there."

I could feel both sets of eyes burning into me.

"Oh wait, maybe I stuck it in this pocket." I opened a small pouch along the side and stuck my hand in. I found a pill bottle, a notepad and finally my fingers brushed metal.

"Ah ha," I said proudly, waving the key in front of me. "I knew I'd find it eventually."

"Yes, well, I've been here for eternity and never leave, so time is all relative to me," the man said.

"You never leave?"

He gave a slight bow. "I am Erasmus Everlasting. I have been the protector of the Vault since its creation and will be here until its destruction."

"Wow," I said. "What do you do for fun?"

Clearly I was out of my mind because my head was killing me and I was making small talk with the guardian of the Vault, who reminded me a lot of that guy in those Thor movies who used his sword to make the heavenly gate appear.

Except this guy was stuck in the Vault until he died. Or was he immortal? Surely he wasn't immortal. If that was the case, then Betty would also be immortal, because as she liked to say, she ran this town.

Hopefully not into its grave.

"My fun is in guarding these items," he said stoically. "This is my life's work, making sure all the precious contents stay secure."

He guided us toward the back wall, where a single keyhole had been constructed in the very center of the ebony structure.

"All keys are to be placed here. If either of you are on the list, then you'll be allowed to enter the inner sanctum. I will guide you to the location of your treasure."

"Treasure?"

Erasmus gave me an amused smile. "There are all manner of things in this place. Some you may see, some you won't."

I pressed at my temples, pushing back on the pressure threatening to swallow every single bit of my attention.

"Let's just make this fast," I said.

Axel shot me a concerned look. "You okay?"

I exhaled a quivering breath. "I don't know how much longer I can take this."

Axel squeezed my shoulder and raised the key. "I'm ready."

Erasmus stepped aside. "Insert at your leisure."

Axel pushed the key into the lock. For a moment nothing happened, and then the outline of the lock flared on the surface surrounding the key. A single line of red light shot up the wall and etched the outline of a box.

Argus's face flashed inside the box, and it was then replaced with another face.

"Your uncle," Axel said.

A man with thinning gray hair, oval spectacles and red cheeks stared down at us. "That's Uncle Donovan?"

"It was him, yeah," Axel said.

Donovan's image disappeared and was replaced by another—Axel.

Erasmus opened his arms. "Congratulations, you have won the lottery."

I gave him a confused look.

"Vault humor," he explained. "It can get very lonely being here all the time."

"But you have help," I said. "I know other people work here."

He nodded. "Yes, but I am the keeper, so it is my job to ensure part of the security. It is my task and one that I take seriously. Besides, I get every other weekend off and every Wednesday."

"Oh, that makes it better. I thought you said you never leave?"

"I tend to exaggerate," he said, blushing.

The onyx wall dissolved, revealing another circular room. Where the outer room had been quiet as a tomb, this one bustled with activity. People milled about dusting shelves, vials, amulet-looking things. A small orb floated through the air, spinning as it made its way around the room.

"What's that?" I said.

"That is a magical baseball that will always give the batter a home run. It's not particularly happy being stuck in the Vault." He leaned over. "It's restless, but we do what we can to exercise it."

As if on cue, one of the associates yanked the ball from the air and started a game of toss with another associate.

"These are all the most magical items in Magnolia Cove?" I said.

Erasmus nodded. "If not the world. Many things here. There's a bag here that will fulfill your every wish. All you have to do is think it, dip your hand in the bag and pull. Next thing you know, voila! You've got a margarita in one hand and a barbecue sandwich in the other."

"Not sure that's what I'd wish for," I said.

Erasmus smiled. "That's the great thing about the bag—each person gets whatever it is he or she wants. It does not discriminate. It's a bottomless pit by nature, but it can also grant wishes."

"And it's here in Magnolia Cove?"

He nodded. "Who would look for it in Alabama? That would be like finding the Holy Grail in the middle of a cotton field."

"Good point," I said.

We wove around the bustling workers and other items that included a tube of glowing lipstick. I wanted to ask what it did, but I figured it would be best not to. I mean, if it made me the most beautiful woman on the planet, I'd be tempted to steal it. Better yet, if it made me look like I'd lost ten pounds overnight and made my pants a little looser around the waist, I might actually kill someone for it.

Just kidding.

Sorta.

I'd at least knock them out and run really fast.

Finally the three of us reached a dark alcove cut into a wall. Erasmus placed a hand on the brick, and it fizzled away, revealing another room lined with boxes.

"This is where you'll find what you're looking for."

"How?" Axel said.

"Drop the key," Erasmus said.

Without hesitation Axel did as he said. The key dropped a foot before zipping halfway across the room. It floated up and down a moment before waving back and forth. It looked like a fish swimming in water. The bow of it was the tail, and the lock end, the head of the creature.

It did that for several seconds before Erasmus crossed to it. The key continued its movement, but it did so faster, as if agitated.

"That's strange," Erasmus said.

"What?" Axel said.

"It appears as if the box the key fits is missing."

My eyebrows shot to peaks. "Missing?"

Erasmus nodded. "Yes. But there's no record of it. If it had been checked out, when the key bonded with the lock in the anteroom, we would have been notified by the screen. But that didn't happen."

Axel's shoulders tightened. He strode forward, fists clenched. "Are you saying the box was stolen?"

Erasmus grimaced. "Unfortunately, that's exactly what I'm saying. I don't know how, but someone managed to enter the Vault and steal the box that belonged to Argus Amulet."

I scoffed. "But how? How could that happen? You're on duty like all the time?"

Erasmus gave me an embarrassed grin. "Perhaps…I was on a potty break?"

TWENTY-ONE

So while Erasmus was on a potty break, the box that held Argus's labradorite had been stolen. It didn't take many guesses for Axel and I to figure out who it could be.

I mean, Samuel was the logical choice, right?

But how had he sneaked inside and pulled it off?

We were in Axel's car, zipping through town. My head throbbed something fierce, and it took all my focus to try to push the pain away.

"Maybe the guy's a better sorcerer than y'all give him credit for. And when I say y'all, I mean the entire town of Magnolia Cove."

Axel gave me a weak smile. "You mean Betty Craple."

I gripped the leather seat as another laboring pain ripped through my noggin. "According to Betty, she knows the thoughts of all the residents."

Axel chuckled. "I don't know why I even bother to find anything out for myself, if she has all the answers."

"That's what I'm saying, too."

As another wave of agony tore into me, I exhaled, focusing on my breath as a way to distract my thoughts.

"You're pale," Axel said.

"I'm surprised I'm not red, the way it hurts so much."

He squeezed my hand. "Don't worry. I'm on my way to Samuel's. We'll grab the labradorite and get you fixed."

I gnawed my bottom lip. Tears sprang to my eyes. "Axel, I don't think I'm going to make it. I can't last that long."

"Hold on, Pepper, we can do it."

At that moment a wave of pain sharp as lightning fissured straight through me. I screamed and crumpled in half. Never in my life had I experienced anything so horrible. It felt like I was splitting in two.

"Hold on, Pepper."

I gripped the dash with fingers of steel. "Where?" I panted. "Where are we going?"

"I'm going to do what I should've done from the very beginning."

"No," I said weakly.

But pain overcame me. I fell back in the seat, writhing and twisting against it. I kept my eyes closed, praying that soon it would be all over. That the torture would disappear and that this nightmare—the one Rufus had caused—would stop.

It seemed like an eternity before Axel came to a screeching halt. I heard him unlock his seat belt and open the door. Next thing I knew, fresh air swallowed me as my door opened.

Axel freed me from the seat belt and scooped me in his arms.

My eyes fluttered open. "Where are we?"

"My house."

I curled my fingers in his shirt. "No, Axel. We're supposed to be in the forest."

He took the steps to his porch as if he was light as air and I weighed nothing more than a feather.

"There was no time to get to the forest. Besides, it's not dark. This is the only shot you've got."

"But Axel," I said weakly.

He opened the front door and pulled me inside. Cold air from the electric unit prickled my skin as it washed over me. We reached the cellar, and he kicked the door open.

Within moments he had a candle lit. He laid me on a fur rug and stroked my hair from my face. He kissed my lips tenderly. If I'd had the energy to drink deeply from him, I would have, but there was nothing left in me. The pain was too much. It stole my drive, and unless Axel moved to erase it, it would soon steal my life.

"Know that I will always care for you," he whispered in my ear. "And there's no time to undress, so let's hope this works."

Before I could respond, he started speaking. The words flew fast and violent from his mouth as if the situation angered him to the point of wanting to slam his fist in a wall.

But instead of hitting brick, Axel spewed the spell in anger. Light hit my eyelids and fluttered open. A golden halo surrounded Axel. Objects near him teetered and fluttered on shelves. A few items crashed to the floor, but then others lifted as if the sorcerer inside him was bending gravity, changing the very magnetic pull around him.

Axel was looking down at the book, and when his gaze met mine, I gasped. The blue eyes that captivated me were no more. In their place were black orbs, resembling those of an animal.

He pointed at me, and the halo washing over him shot out, roping me like Wonder Woman's freakin' lasso.

Pinned by the binds, I could only watch as Axel began to morph into the beast. At the same time I felt the spell tying me to Rufus go slack. I could feel the line tethered between me and the sorcerer die bit by bit as I watched the man I cared for die in a different way.

He wasn't physically dying, but his body did as Axel shifted hair by hair and bone by bone into the beast.

His forearms stretched and sprouted fur. The shirt on his back split open, revealing a chest twice its normal size. His jeans ripped and shredded.

And all the while I could only stare helplessly. In the middle of it all, Axel panted heavily.

The magical words rushing from him at an accelerated rate stopped.

He looked at me. The beast was like seriously in him. What I mean was, Axel was still there, but I knew that within moments he would be lost and all that would remain was the werewolf.

"Pepper," he said in a gravelly voice, "you're almost free."

"Stop," I said, trying to reach for him. "The headache's nearly gone. You can stop this."

He shook his head. "In a few moments I'll be done. When that happens, the rope around you will disappear. At that point, there's one thing I need you to do."

Tears stung my eyes. "What?" I said hoarsely.

"Run."

"Don't," I pleaded.

He took my hand. "Promise me you will find the strength to run."

The headache had zapped a lot of energy from me. "I don't know."

"Promise, me," he insisted.

I swallowed down a knot of emotions and nodded. "I will."

Axel turned around and faced the opposite direction. He spoke again, and this time the intensity jacked up like a thousand and one degrees while his transformation quickened.

As I watched Axel's body lengthen and morph into something completely different, I felt the last bit of connection to Rufus die. I waited for it to peter out into nothing.

It did so with an audible *snap.*

In hindsight I don't really know whether that was the spell or simply Axel's body making one final adjustment before he morphed completely into the beast.

Either way, the lasso roped around me dissolved. I fell to the floor with a *thud*. My headache was completely gone, thank goodness, but before me stood a massive, towering, flesh-eating werewolf. The wolf was three times larger than Axel had been as a man. I likened his beast form to the Incredible Hulk of werewolves. No joke. He was that big.

The sound caught the beast's attention. Axel in wolf form flipped around. Dark eyes met mine, and a primal wave of fear flooded every single cell in my body.

I scrambled to my feet and did the one thing he'd said to do.

I ran.

TWENTY-TWO

I flew up the stairs and threw the door shut. I could hear the wolf's steps at my back. My only hope of making it out of the house alive was that the doorways would be too small for him to maneuver, and if they didn't stop him, they'd at least slow him down.

Like any too-stupid-to-live heroine in a horror flick, I turned my head when I reached the hall.

The cellar door flew open. The beast was lodged in the frame, his shoulders too wide to fit through. I saw him push and heard wood splinter as he shoved his way from the cellar.

I had to get out and warn everyone. Let the people know that Axel was loose—before anyone got hurt.

As the beast pushed, I reached the front door. Thank God Axel hadn't locked it. My fingers trembled; my knees shook. If I'd had to work a stupid chain lock, I would probably have been dead by now.

Just as I pulled the door open, the beast smashed free of the cellar. I yelped as I yanked the door shut and ran for the car. Axel's Mustang was a stick shift, and even though I was a little bit country and had ridden on my grandpa's tractor a time or two, and had even kissed my first boyfriend between shifting gears in his ancient pickup truck, I wasn't good enough at clutching and shifting gears to make it into town without killing the engine.

And thus I'd probably be eaten by a werewolf before I got there.

So the truck it was.

The door was unlocked. I jumped in the cab and looked for keys. None. There also wasn't a push button to start the engine.

Holy smokes. I was in deep doo-doo.

What was I going to do? Maybe the wolf would be stuck inside the house and wouldn't be able to escape. I *had* shut the door behind me, and the beast had claws. It's not as if he had thumbs that would help him turn a knob. That wasn't going to happen.

That meant my only choice was to get out, find the nearest neighbor and use their phone. It seemed my one and only option.

I grabbed the handle and pushed open the door when a crash caught my attention.

My gaze darted up to the house, where a front window had been shattered.

"Holy shrimp and grits."

The beast stood on the lawn, shaking out his coat.

"Son of a gun."

The animal had jumped through the window and now stood on the grass, staring directly at me with gleaming black eyes.

For a second I thought Axel lived in the beast somewhere. That it might just run off in the opposite direction when he realized it was me, Pepper.

But oh, y'all, I was so wrong.

The wolf launched straight for me. Before I even realized what I was doing, I placed my hands on the dash and shoved all the fear and anxiety I'd been experiencing the last few days into the truck.

Magic buzzed from my skin over the plastic and seeped inside. It was like watching a sponge soak up milk. Not that my power was white—it wasn't; it was sort of like a bluish film that I couldn't really see, but I could sense and feel.

Then the most miraculous thing happened—the engine roared to life.

And it was just in time. The werewolf bounded onto the hood. I hit the gearshift into reverse and backed down the gravel drive at a speed somewhere between reckless and death-wish.

Luckily it was closer to reckless.

I swung onto the road, hitting the brakes so fast the wolf tumbled off the hood and onto the ground.

I slammed the stick into drive and barreled down the road. I shot a quick look into the rearview. The wolf rose, shook its head and took off following me.

I gunned the engine and laid on the horn. It was the closest thing I had to a siren. My mind raced. There was only one place I could think of to go—the one building where there were enough people that might be able to stop the wolf.

The police station.

As I approached the heart of downtown, I blared the horn, trying to get as many people's attention as possible.

Luckily it was later in the afternoon and people had already left work and had headed home. Traffic was light, and those who saw me coming—hazard lights blinking and horn roaring—stopped.

I saw their looks of horror, and a chill swept over me. Or maybe that was just adrenaline soaking my body with the jitters.

Yep, probably that was it.

This wasn't like a high speed chase in an action movie where my vehicle swerves left and right, avoiding cars while people jump out of the way.

No. Magnolia Cove is a quiet town. Folks saw me coming or heard me about a half a mile away so that by the time I reached the busier intersections, people were already waiting to see who the heck was making so much noise and why.

I passed a woman in yoga pants walking her little shih tzu familiar. I even passed Betty Craple, who waved her corncob pipe at me. I pivoted my head and saw her get a good solid look at the werewolf and then take off sprinting behind me.

Lord yes, Betty Craple could've run in a geriatric marathon if she'd wanted.

Grandma might've won, too.

I kept my eye on the creature, making sure he was chasing me and hadn't veered off when he saw something else. Luckily I didn't have to worry. Maybe it was the horn blaring, or maybe he was like most animals and was simply attracted to bright, shiny objects, like me.

To me, bright and shiny means diamonds and jewelry. In the wolf's case, the pickup was shiny and loud.

Finally I saw the police station ahead.

If I parked in the lot and jumped out, I'd never reach the doors in time. The wolf would have me in his jaws before I pulled the handle to get inside.

The only option was to jump the curb, get up on the sidewalk and either open the truck door and death roll out, or jump the curb, stop the vehicle and run for the door, praying the whole way that I beat the wolf into the station.

And maybe Betty would call ahead with magic. Heck, I didn't have a phone, but that little lady had more power in one of her boobs than I had in my whole body. I wasn't one hundred percent sure of that, but I was pretty darned positive.

That hunch turned out to be correct.

Right as the vehicle lurched over the concrete curb, a half a dozen officers streamed out of the station, hands raised, magic ready to take down Axel.

And as much as that's what was needed, I suddenly felt very protective of him.

"No," I said to no one. "You can't hurt him."

The truck swerved as I hit the grass surrounding the station. I yanked the steering wheel to the right, and the tail swung wide. I was going so fast, and I hadn't dropped my speed enough to avoid what happened next.

The truck bed slammed into the brick building. The crunch of metal filled my ears as the vehicle twisted and warped from the impact. My nerve endings were on fire from the adrenaline flooding my body. I looked in the rearview to see a man-sized hole had been bored into the station.

I could see Rufus smiling from his cell.

But I didn't have time to process the meaning of that because the next thing I knew, the officers were aiming their magic at Axel in wolf form.

Threads of magic shot into his fur. The wolf must've been high on adrenaline too, because he acted like the power feeding into him was nothing more than an inconvenience.

And the animal was still barreling down on me.

I shifted over the bucket seat to the passenger's side. I opened the door and fell from the cab.

The officers had increased their power. The wolf had paused but still wasn't down.

Which was what I knew they wanted.

After scrambling to my feet, I raced past the officers into the station. I figured it was the safest place to be. Let them capture the creature. They had more experience with this sort of thing than I did, anyway.

Dust and debris filled the station from where the truck had burst through the wall. I coughed, waving away the particles. I pressed my face to the glass and watched the scene unfold.

"Looks like your boyfriend went rogue."

A fissure of anger raced down my back. I slowly turned to see the smug expression on Rufus's face. I returned to glancing out the window.

The wolf had turned on the officers. He spat and snarled, leaping onto one of the men.

"No," I yelled.

"That's what happens when a monster is unleashed on a poor suspecting town like this one," Rufus said. "You can hide a monster. You can even bury it, but eventually it will rear its ugly head. That's just how it goes."

I turned on him. "You. You're the one who did this. You created this havoc just so you could laugh about it."

"*Moi?*" he said in a terrible French accent. His gaze swept from my feet to my head. "Why would I do that when all I needed was to walk in and take what I wanted?"

"Axel broke your stupid spell. He's stuck in that form for Lord knows how long."

The officers had managed to free their friend from the wolf's grasp. He looked unharmed. The wolf wasn't retreating, and the men were still trying to bring it down with magic, which clearly wasn't having any impact on the creature.

From the distance another slew of officers appeared, led by Garrick Young. My stomach clenched. Garrick and Axel were friends from way back, he wouldn't want to hurt his friend—but if Garrick had no choice, he'd do what was needed to keep Magnolia Cove safe.

"Don't worry," Rufus said. "I'm sure they'll have no problem containing that beast. Of course, they'll probably have to get a silver bullet to do so, but then there goes your boyfriend. What a pity. Gone at the hands of the very people he called 'friends.'"

I whirled on him. "You are a horrible person. Just shut up! *Shut up!*"

Rufus smirked. "You think it's so terrible to want to live in the place that kicked me out?"

It infuriated me that he wouldn't just shut the heck up. I wanted to walk over to the cell and slap him upside his head. But instead I stared at the wolf and the men surrounding him.

Rufus didn't stop. "These people threw me out. Me. The greatest sorcerer they'd ever seen. They got rid of me, left me outside the walls to rot without offering a chance to redeem myself."

"You play *vampire* on people. What's there to redeem?"

He chuckled. "That's only one side. The side that believes what I do is for evil. I'm not trying to hurt anyone. I want these people to flourish, to be more than the measly peasants they are."

Peasants? Who was he? King of the world?

"What makes you think anyone wants your help?" I finally said.

"We're witches, Pepper. Witches, wizards and sorcerers, but we're still racked with disease, have arthritis, grow old."

I frowned. "In other words, live a human life?"

"Yes! Why? Why are we doing that when we could tap unimaginable power? You, for instance. You could bend metal, build buildings, destroy anything you wanted—with your mind. You're only hindered by what you believe hinders you. And what are you doing? Running a familiar shop in the middle of a cotton field."

"I like my shop," I said rather pathetically.

Because I mean, since he put it that way, he made us sound like demigods. Like more than what we were.

"You're acting like we're superheroes," I pointed out.

"*We are.* Now you're getting it. But we're bound by what's dictated to us. By myself, I don't have the power to do half the things I know I could be capable of. But with help, I could."

"What help? *My* help? No way, Jose. You can hit the road on that thought, Jack."

"My name is Rufus."

I nearly slapped my forehead. For someone so smart, or so evil, boy did he lack common sense. Or at least a working knowledge of popular culture.

I was about to tell him that when a blast from a shotgun rang in the sky. My gaze swiveled to the scene on the lawn.

Garrick stood, shotgun raised and aimed at the creature. I stared at Axel, praying to all that was good in the world that he hadn't been hit because I had no doubt of what was in that barrel—silver bullets.

The werewolf whirled toward the men. He looked unharmed. I released a breath.

"And the moment I've been waiting for has arrived," Rufus said.

I didn't know if somehow Rufus manipulated the scene the way he wanted or if luck simply worked in his cotton-picking favor, but what happened next made the blood pool at my feet.

Garrick shot again, this time hitting the werewolf in the hip. I screamed. The wolf tumbled back with such a force that the beast crashed into the building beside the hole that the truck had made.

The station exterior, probably already weakened from the initial damage, collapsed as the creature shot inside with such a force that he hit Rufus's cell.

The bars caved in a shower of dust and plaster.

Before the police could rush inside, Rufus stepped out of his cell. He straightened the collar of his jacket, smiled at me and said, "Good luck."

With that, he snapped his fingers and disappeared.

TWENTY-THREE

There was little time to process what had happened with Rufus because at that moment the werewolf gazed up at me. His dark eyes met mine, and my breath hitched.

I narrowed my gaze until I felt my brows pinch. "Axel? I know you're in there. You have to be."

The wolf stared at me. I reached out again. I mean, I can communicate with animals, y'all. There's no reason why I shouldn't be able to communicate with Axel in his werewolf form. Surely somewhere deep in his consciousness there was a tiny piece that remembered who he truly was—not a beast but a good man. A solid man. One who would fight pretty hard, if not to the death, for me.

Okay, maybe I was jumping ahead on his feelings, there. But I felt in my gut that the connection between us dug deeper than on the human level. If I tried, I felt I could connect with the beast.

"Axel?" I said again.

The beast cringed, and in that moment I knew somewhere in his mind that Axel had heard me.

Or perhaps it was the wound in his side.

I stepped forward, hand outstretched. "Axel?"

He craned his neck as if to sniff my hand.

Right then, Garrick Young and company barreled into the station. "Grab him! Throw a rope around him!"

The werewolf jumped to his feet, shook his head and launched himself through the hole.

He dashed to the left, into a copse of trees, and vanished from sight.

I whirled on Garrick. "He's wounded. We have to go after him."

The sheriff grabbed my arms. "I hit him with a sonic blast, not an actual bullet. He's not wounded, but I hoped it would be enough to knock him out."

Garrick turned to his men. "Sound the alarm. Get everyone inside their homes. There's a dangerous beast loose in Magnolia Cove. I want officers on the perimeter. I need a spell. A bubble spell."

Another man said, "I'm on it."

Anger blazed on Garrick's face. "No one leaves Magnolia Cove and no one enters. You understand?"

The officer nodded. "Got it."

In that instant Betty Craple marched through the hole that the werewolf had created. She shoved up her sleeves. "Y'all need some help working a containment spell?"

Garrick pulled off his hat and swiped away the line of sweat covering his forehead. "Help would be great."

"But wait," I said. "Rufus is gone. He's going somewhere—"

And then it hit me exactly where he was headed.

"That nuisance is the least of our problems," Garrick said. "We've got Axel in full wolf loose in town. That's my main concern."

"I don't think he'll hurt anyone," I said. I didn't know how I knew this, but I felt it. It was like a remnant from the moment I'd connected with Axel. "Not unless he's cornered."

Okay, so yes, the wolf had chased me from the house to the station. Yes, he's snapped and snarled. But when he'd been lying on the floor, hurt and dazed, I'd touched him. I knew I had. Maybe in that moment I'd reached the real Axel somewhere underneath. Perhaps he'd awoken inside the beast enough to hold on to his consciousness, remember who he was and not hurt anyone.

Of course, he'd run off, so that didn't help.

"He's a werewolf, ma'am," another officer said. "If you've met one, you've met 'em all. Feral as they come. They'll kill whoever, whenever they can."

"Garrick?" I said, tears filling my eyes. "Promise me you won't hurt him."

Garrick squeezed my shoulder in a sort of brotherly way. "I'll do my best, but Pepper, if Axel hurts anyone, he'll be giving in to the very fears this community already has about him. The fact that he's even running wild doesn't bode well for his future here."

I started to crumple but remembered I had to be strong. There were things to do, and I had to do them. The police couldn't help me, which meant I was on my own.

At that moment my aunts Mint and Licky walked into the station.

A slow, curling smile crept over my face. My aunts were chaos witches, which meant havoc and mayhem followed everywhere they went. Which also meant that for what I needed to do, they would be perfect partners in crime.

"What the heck happened here?" Mint said.

"Looks like a tornado hit the place," Licky added.

I grabbed my aunts by their elbows. "Listen, I need your help."

"Anything," Mint said.

We stepped outside. Suddenly a siren blared to life. At the same time a bluish shield appeared in the sky.

"We're trapped," Mint said.

Garrick's voice boomed over the town. "People of Magnolia Cove. You are on lockdown. There is a dangerous werewolf loose inside our walls. Please do not attempt to take this creature on your own. If you see him, report his presence to the police immediately. But remember, do not engage on your own. The creature is highly dangerous."

"Oh," Mint said, "sounds like we've got a real problem."

"You don't even know the half of it," I said. "But I need your help."

"Are we going back to Betty's for facials?" Licky said, wide-eyed. She was Amelia's mother and the character resemblance was pretty spot-on. They were so much alike it was almost scary.

"We're going to the house to grab Hugo, my dragon," I said. "But after that, we've got two places to go."

"Why?" Mint said.

I nearly growled my next words. "Because we need to stop Rufus from destroying this town. To do that, we need a block of labradorite."

"Do you know where to find it?" Licky said.

I gazed up at the bluish sky. A pang of fear pinged my heart. Axel would not be safe—not until I had the stone and we'd gotten rid of Rufus.

I ground my teeth and said, "Yes. I know exactly where to find it."

TWENTY-FOUR

*M*int and Licky each hooked an arm around my elbow. "What are we doing?" I said.

Mint laughed. "There's more than one way to fly through the air."

Confused, I said, "There is?"

Licky nodded. "Mint and I've been doing this for years. Before our mother ever let us get our cast-iron skillets, we'd sneak out a window at night and fly around town to see our boyfriends."

"Boy, you two were a handful, weren't you?"

Mint winked at me. "Still are."

With that, we lifted into the air. I pedaled my feet as if riding an invisible bicycle because it was very weird and I didn't know what to do with my limbs.

"Hang on," Licky said. "We go fast."

She wasn't kidding. We dashed through the air at top speed. The wind blew my hair, and boy, was I going to need a hairbrush by the time we got to the house. But unfortunately there wasn't going to be time for beauty.

We landed on the sidewalk about two minutes later. "Thank you," I said.

We dashed inside the house and found Amelia and Cordelia pacing the room.

"What's going on?" Amelia said.

"Axel broke Rufus's curse on me. He's now a werewolf and running loose in town. Rufus is also loose. The police are after Axel, but we've got to stop Rufus before it's too late."

Concern slashed over Cordelia's face. "Why?"

"Because he wants to ruin this town. He's angry and out for revenge. I need Hugo. He might be able to help."

Amelia shot Cordelia a look. "And what about us? We want to help, too."

I gnawed my bottom lip. "I don't want anyone to be hurt. This is dangerous."

Amelia fisted her hands to her hips. "Hey, we're the sweet tea witches. We stick together through thick and thin."

Cordelia nodded in agreement.

I shrugged. "Okay, then. The more the merrier. Let me grab Hugo. Where is he?"

"In his cage, I think," Amelia said.

I raced upstairs and took the sleeping dragon from his cage. "Wake up, boy. I need your help today."

"Mama," he said.

I pulled him out and placed him on my shoulders.

"Where you going, sugar?" Mattie said from the window seat.

"Mattie, I'm so glad you're here."

She stretched. "Sounds like there's trouble."

"You wouldn't believe it. Listen, I need you to get a message to Betty. She's at the police station. Think you can do that?"

She blinked at me. "Since she doesn't own a cell phone, I'll do it."

"Great."

I gave her the message and opened the window so she could scamper down the roof and onto the ground.

"Be careful," I said. "There's a werewolf on the loose."

Mattie laughed. "Everyone knows wolves can't climb trees."

"Then you'll be just fine."

When I got back downstairs, Mint, Licky, Cordelia and Amelia stood waiting.

I exhaled a deep shot of air. Nerves raced through my body, firing all over. It made me feel like I'd received some sort of jacked-up adrenaline shot. My fingers trembled and my knees were jelly, but I ignored it. There was a lot of work to do and very little time.

I forced a confident smile and said, "Okay, this is what we're going to do."

~

"I KNOW you're in there, Amulet! I've got the key to that box."

We reached Samuel Amulet's house a short time later. I'd knocked on the door several times, but Amulet hadn't answered. My hopes had crashed to the ground, but then Licky said something that lifted them.

"He just opened a curtain on the top floor and looked down."

"So he's ignoring us?" I said.

"Appears so," Mint said. She cracked her knuckles. "Want Licky and I to make him so hot he thinks it's cooler outside than in?"

I swiped an arm across my head, removing a sheet of sweat. "It's as humid as the jungle today. Only an idiot would think he'd be better off out here."

Licky clapped her hands. "How about a good old-fashioned itching spell? The best ones are those we place down a person's pants."

I held up a hand. "That's not going to happen. No. I'm going for something nice and easy."

"What's that?" Amelia said.

I smiled. "Good old-fashioned scare tactics." I stepped off the porch and down to the walkway. "Amulet, I've got a dragon ready to burn down your house if you don't open this door right now. I've got the key. I only need the labradorite for a few minutes. Then you can have it back."

Finally I heard the *snick* of a lock. Samuel peeked his head out from the door. He eyed the four of us plus one dragon. "You promise to give it back?"

I nodded. "Listen, all of Magnolia Cove needs this right now. Please."

He ushered us inside. The interior was dark and smelled of old people. Lace doilies were draped over every bare surface, even the drapes.

"You live here?" Cordelia said.

"Inherited it from my grandparents. I'm not much for decorating," he said.

"Obviously," Amelia said quietly.

He led us to a round side table and whipped yet another doily from a square shape, revealing a colorful blue and green box with the same etching as the key.

"That's the one I saw at the Vault," Amelia said.

I dragged my gaze to Samuel. "How'd you manage to steal it?"

Samuel swiped a finger over his lips. "Let's just say I have connections—someone inside helped me out."

"Oh, they could be fired for that," Amelia said.

Samuel shot her a scathing look. "I know. That's why I'm not saying who it is."

"That's good," she added, "because they could be arrested, thrown in jail, and that's *after* they lose their job."

I rolled my eyes. "Let's just get on with it. There's not much time."

I pulled the key from my pocket. Lord, was I thankful that I'd snagged it back from Axel after leaving the Vault. If I hadn't, I wouldn't even know where to begin looking for it.

I held my breath as I pushed the key inside the lock and turned. The tumblers flipped, and the key moved easily. The lock sprang, and the lid popped slightly.

I peeled back the cover, and there it was. The rock of labradorite was easily one of the most beautiful stones I'd ever seen. Veins of aqua and green roped over darker hues of blue and black. It was absolutely breathtaking.

"So that's it," I whispered.

Samuel leaned over so far a line of drool dripped from his mouth.

"Gross," I said. "Get a grip."

He wiped it away. "Sorry, but I've waited so long for it to be mine."

Before he could grab it, I snatched the stone. Raw energy swirled inside the thing. I could feel it living, nearly breathing just below the surface of the stone. Oh yes, we needed this. Without it, we'd be lost.

"You'll be waiting a hair longer. A deal's a deal—unless you want to face off against Hugo, there. He might look young, but he can barbecue just about anything."

Samuel shrank back. "No, no. Take it. I trust you."

I squeezed his shoulder. "Thank you."

I opened my purse and laid the stone inside. Let me tell you, that block of rock wasn't light. I hugged the bag to my chest, and we left. Once outside, I hopped on my skillet and turned to look at my family.

"Everyone ready?" I said.

They all nodded.

"Let's go."

The five of us lifted off from the ground. Hugo flew in the air beside me, following along like an obedient familiar, which is what he pretty much was.

When we landed at our destination, worry immediately filled me.

"What in holy heck?" Amelia said, touching down.

"That's going to be a problem," Cordelia said. "Too bad Zach's not here to help. With all his mystical knowledge of history, I bet he'd have a solution."

I shot her a hopeful look. "Can you call him?"

She nodded. "I think he hates me, but I'll do it." My cousin pulled out her phone. "Let's hope he's still in town."

"Fingers crossed," Amelia said.

I stared at the twin lions guarding the Vault. They paced back and forth, growling and snarling. I'd made it past them one time before, so I wouldn't have been worried if it hadn't been for the red stuff dripping from their mouths.

"Is that blood?" Amelia said.

A shot of panic zipped down my spine. "That's what it looks like. Oh dear Lord, what did they kill?"

"More like who?" Licky said.

Cordelia strolled back. "Zach's already left town. He can't get back in."

"Great," I said, "'cause it looks like we've got carnivorous lions on our hands."

Mint squinted at the scene. She pointed at something. "Is that a tomato?"

"Where?" I said.

"There."

I followed the line of her finger until I noticed a partially squashed tomato on the ground. One of the lions walked over, sniffed it, and gobbled it in one swallow.

I leaned back. "Since when did lions start liking tomatoes?"

"Maybe they're vegetarians," Amelia said.

"Never heard of such a thing."

"Everyone knows lions eat people," Licky said.

Cordelia placed a hand on my arm. "Zach said that. He said they might eat fruit and to try it. Tomatoes are technically a fruit since they have seeds."

I glanced at my family. "Mint, Licky—you got this?"

Mint cracked her knuckles. "We ain't chaos witches for nothing."

I grimaced. This could go wrong in so many ways. Actually, anything involving my aunts could. "Just don't get killed."

Licky smacked her lips. "Promise."

Mint clapped her hands, and a basket of tomatoes instantly appeared in her arms. "Hey, boys, we've got your tomatoes right here."

The lions glanced over, not appearing interested.

Licky grabbed one of the tomatoes and threw it at one of the animals' feet. The fruit smashed, creating a red streak on the concrete. The lion leaned over, sniffed and gobbled it up.

The second lion padded over and growled. My aunts took that as an invitation to start throwing tomatoes at the beasts' feet. As fast as the fruit smashed to the ground, the lions ate them up.

"Lead them away from the entrance," I said.

My aunts did, throwing the tomatoes over to the side. The lions followed, eating the trail of ruined fruit.

I glanced at my cousins. "The coast is clear. Come on."

With the lions' backs completely to us, I led Amelia and Cordelia past them and up the steps to the Vault.

The door opened easily and closed quietly behind us. We stood in the outer chamber. The circular room was eerily quiet.

"Something's very wrong," Amelia said.

"You've got that right."

My head swung right. Tacked to the wall and secured with some kind of molten metal bars, stood Erasmus.

I rushed over. "Are you okay?"

He nodded. "I am fine. Nothing a little Jack Daniels can't fix."

I grabbed one of the metal bars and pulled, but nothing happened. "You're stuck. I don't know if I can get you out."

He shook his head. "If you can defeat Rufus, this will go away. It will vanish along with the sorcerer's spell that has me trapped."

"But you're not hurt?" Amelia said.

Erasmus shook his head. "I am not hurt. Now go. Stop Rufus before he finds what it is he wants."

"What does he want?" I said.

"The bottomless bag. I believe he wants to use it to put Magnolia Cove inside and swallow us all."

I frowned. "Is that even possible?"

Erasmus shrugged. "It is bottomless."

"But the neck of it isn't that big. It can't swallow a city."

He stared at me with eyes full of fear. "The neck is adjustable."

"Oh dear Lord," I said to my cousins. "Come on, let's get Rufus."

We turned to head into the Vault's inner sanctum but stopped dead in our tracks.

Rufus stood at the entrance, a burlap sack in one hand. The other hand held his signature blue flame.

He smiled wickedly. "Hey, ladies. Thank you for joining me. So glad you're here. Now let's have some fun."

TWENTY-FIVE

*R*ufus kicked aside a piece of twisted metal that must've been left over from his tussle with Erasmus.

"You've come just in time," he said.

"In time for what?"

His lips curled into a serpentine grin. "In time to watch the fall of Magnolia Cove, the bane of my existence."

I rolled my eyes. "Please. Aren't you getting carried away? I mean, isn't it the other way around? Aren't *you* the bane of Magnolia Cove's existence? You're like a spider that won't die no matter how hard you swat it with a newspaper."

"Magazines are better," Amelia said. "More weight to them."

Cordelia nodded. "Or even a hardback book. Not one of your own, you don't want to ruin it. But the ones from the library have that nice protective cover that wipes clean. That's a much better choice for spider killing."

"Will the three of you shut up?" he shouted, red-faced.

"We were only discussing the finer points of spider killing," I said. "One day, you might need our tips and tricks."

"I don't need your help with anything," he said. "I have everything I need right here. Behold, the sack of doom!"

I yawned. "All this talk has been great, but I've got a werewolf to help catch after this, so do you mind surrendering now?"

Rufus gave a belly laugh so deep it nearly shook the walls. "Surrender? Me? Don't you have that the other way around? You should be surrendering, because once this is over, you're coming with me. This time, no one will break the spell I place on you because there won't be anyone to save you."

"That sounds very scary," I said. "But I don't think that's going to happen."

Rufus cackled. "What are you going to do about it? You don't even know how to touch the power at your fingertips."

I opened my purse and pulled out the labradorite, presenting it to him. "I don't need to. I have this."

His eyes flared. "That still won't help you."

I smirked and reached into my bag again. This time, I lifted out the hat that Sylvia had loaned me. "And I also have this." I placed it atop my head and said, "Time for all of this to end, Rufus."

"Good luck," he said, raising the hand holding the blue orb.

"She won't need luck," shot out another voice from behind us.

I didn't have to look to know it was Betty. But it did help that out of the corner of my eye, I saw her and Sylvia Spirits come into view.

I handed Betty the labradorite. "I assume you know how to use this?"

She took it. "I've got an idea."

"This has been a nice party, but I'm afraid I'm beginning to feel a bit like a rooster in a henhouse."

"I'm still here," Erasmus said. "You're not the only man in the room."

Rufus smirked. "I'm the only one potent enough to do anything."

"That stings," Erasmus said.

"Enough," Betty said. "Rufus, it's time for you to go away and not come back."

He threw the orb right at me. I sure as heck didn't know how the hat worked, but I wanted the ball to stop. I focused on that.

The blue light's path halted about three inches from my face. I stared at it. The magic was a swirl of white and robin's-egg blue. It was so pretty. I decided that it couldn't hurt me if I didn't let it, so I snatched it from the air. It was cold to the touch, and a mist wafted off it. I stared at the orb for a moment before throwing it back to Rufus.

The orb struck his feet. Apparently I needed to work out more because I was aiming for his chest and threw short.

An explosion filled the Vault. Rufus staggered back. He lifted the bag. The burlap mouth yawned open. Erasmus had not been kidding when he said it was adjustable.

As the mouth opened to swallow the Vault and all of us, Betty and Sylvia placed their hands on the labradorite. A yellow beam shot out as they chanted.

The light flared toward Rufus. He placed the bag in front of him as if creating a shield, but the magic inside the labradorite was too strong. It blasted right through the bag and surrounded him.

Rufus struggled. He fought the light, kicking and punching. "This won't be the last you see of me," he shouted.

Just then the light blipped off and Rufus disappeared. The bag dropped to the floor, its mouth shrinking back to normal size.

I exhaled a deep shot of air. I glanced at my family. "Everyone okay?"

They all nodded. "We were lucky he only threw that one light. I'm surprised he didn't strike earlier," I said.

Betty spit on the labradorite and polished it with her sleeve. "Guy likes to talk. Thinks he's so superior. I believe he thought he'd get that bag to swallow us before we could successfully use the stone against him. Shows what he knew."

I smiled. "Thank goodness."

"Where is he?" Amelia said.

Betty handed the labradorite back to me. "We sent him out of town and used the labradorite to add an extra layer of security against him entering. I don't know how long it'll hold, but should be long enough for us to work out a new spell, one that's hopefully Rufus-proof."

Amelia pressed a finger to her cheek. "It's too bad you couldn't send him into something like they did in that old *Superman II* movie.

You know, where the bad guys are in that other dimension and then a rocket or something shatters the glass and they're set free?"

Cordelia flicked dirt out from under her fingernails. "Then a rocket would free Rufus, so he'd show up again."

"Oh, right," Amelia said, clearly depressed her idea wasn't snatched up as fool-proof.

I glanced at the Sylvia. "But where's Barnaby?"

Sylvia shook her head. "I called, but there wasn't an answer."

I cracked my knuckles. "I need to find him. He can tell me how to use the stone to free Axel. I've got to get out of here."

Erasmus called out from his metal prison. "I'm still stuck here. Anytime one of y'all wants to get me out, I'd be happy to be free of these confines. In fact, I may take my leave from the Vault for a while. Too much drama."

I bit back a laugh. "You have this covered?" I said to Betty.

Her answer was to snort magical sparkles from her nose. They wrapped around the twisted metal, bending it away from Erasmus. The sound was worse than a thousand fingernails grating down an old-fashioned chalkboard.

Ignoring the sound, I rushed from the building, shouting as I went, "Y'all wish me luck."

There would be plenty for them to do. Rufus had wrecked the inside of the Vault in his search for the bag. There would be cleanup and then some. Besides, I could perform the next part of my duty by myself. I knew I could communicate with Axel. All I had to do was find him, and for that I needed Barnaby.

As I headed out the door, I prayed the wizard was safe.

TWENTY-SIX

I left everyone behind, even Hugo. The dragon was still too young to face off against a werewolf, and even though he wanted to come, I handed him to Licky and made her promise to keep him safe.

My aunts, by the way, had the lions eating out of their palms—literally. The magical creatures were gorging on tomatoes handed to them straight from my aunts.

Gross.

Now I know plenty of y'all can eat a tomato like an apple, but the thought of that makes me want to retch. I like ketchup. I like salsa. I do not like raw tomatoes.

Ew.

I jumped on my skillet and flew to Barnaby's house. Lockdown or no lockdown, I was not about to let the police take down a werewolf without me at least trying to return him to his true form. Besides, the sooner I saved Axel, the less likely it would be that someone would get hurt.

If Axel attacked anyone in his wolf form, he'd never forgive himself—I was absolutely certain of that. So I needed to get to Barnaby's and quick.

After all, Sylvia had told me that when I had the labradorite, Barnaby could help free Axel.

Which was why when I arrived at Barnaby's house, I didn't wait for an invitation to enter. I threw open the door and rushed inside.

"Barnaby," I yelled.

I careened into the pocket doors the led to the sitting room. I shoved them aside and gasped.

Barnaby lay on the chaise lounge, his head lolled back. Rubber tubing had been roped around his arm. Delilah leaned over him, a syringe in her hand.

A bottle labeled MORPHINE lay on the table. Delilah glanced up at me, a look of panic scrolling across her features.

Luckily her needle hadn't been emptied into Barnaby's vein yet.

"He asked me to do it," she said quickly.

"Like heck he did," I said. "You must think I was born this morning."

Her face twisted into a strangely sick smile.

"You killed Argus," I said, "and that other woman whose name escapes me because I didn't know her."

"Ingrid Gale," she said.

"Thank you. But, why?"

Delilah shivered with what appeared to be some sort of sick pleasure. "I love the look on their faces when they pass. Argus didn't have that peaceful appearance since I used the deadly nightshade on him, but my father will."

I shook my head. Of course I'd heard of caretakers and nurses killing patients, but I never expected to meet one—let alone walk in on her when she was about to murder.

It was sick and creepy.

"But why?"

"I love to kill. It's simply within me. I delight in death, Pepper. What can I say? I have a problem."

"I would say you definitely have a problem."

She pricked her finger on the tip of the needle. "Too bad you won't live to tell anyone."

Delilah flew at me, the needle aimed to plunge into my neck. Feeling a surge of power similar to what I'd felt when I faced off against Rufus, I raised my hand.

Delilah paused in midair.

At that moment Barnaby awoke. "Huh? What's going on in here? Pepper, why are you working magic against my daughter?"

I nodded toward the morphine and the needle. "Because your daughter was about to take your life, Mr. Battle."

"It wasn't me," Delilah said. "It's her, Daddy. She's the one holding me hostage."

For the briefest of seconds panic flared in my chest. "It wasn't me. Barnaby, I promise you. I'm not the one holding the needle. Delilah admitted to me that she killed Argus and was going to kill you."

Barnaby glanced from me to his daughter. He raised his hands, and like a conductor leading an orchestra, the wizard completed a series of movements.

Barnaby spoke. "Delilah, you forget that I see what happened a few minutes ago if I'm in the room—conscious or unconscious."

I watched as time moved backward. I saw what I can only describe as an astral projection or ghost of myself talking to Delilah.

The projection, which is the best description I can give of the scene that unfolded before me, showed me barging into the room, finding Delilah over Barnaby's unconscious body and admitting everyone.

The panic I had felt dissolved.

Barnaby watched in silence and then continued to remain quiet for another minute. All the while I was thinking we really needed to get this show on the road because, you know, man-killing werewolf on the loose, cops ready to kill him at any moment.

Yeah, all that stuff.

Barnaby stared at the bottle for a long time. "How could you do that, Delilah?"

Delilah couldn't move her limbs, but she could manipulate her mouth. "I'm sorry, Father, but I can't help it."

Barnaby rose, yanked the rubber tubing from his arm and tossed it across the floor. He straightened his collar and crossed to face his daughter. "I will have you arrested shortly. I do not pretend to understand any of this. I do not understand why you would take advantage of me while I was sleeping, and I will mourn this, but not now."

Delilah, I suppose realizing she was caught and there was no way out of the situation, gritted her teeth. "I can't help it. I'm a monster. Lock me up, throw away the key and all that; otherwise, I'll only strike again."

I locked gazes with Barnaby. "Mayor Battle, Magnolia Cove needs you. I have the labradorite. Rufus is gone. Betty and Sylvia removed him from town, and not a minute too soon. Axel's a werewolf. Sylvia said you might be able to help change him back."

Barnaby grabbed his keys. "I do believe I can." He led me toward the front door. "Get me up to speed."

I smiled. "The entire police force is after Axel. I don't know if they've caught him or not, because I was busy trying to save this town from Rufus while they were all out chasing him."

Barnaby opened the door. I stepped through. He took a long look at Delilah before pointing a finger at her. A stream of magic flowed from the digit, encasing her already frozen form.

"That should keep you until we get back," he said.

With that, the two of us left the house. The sun was setting and night was only minutes away from completely swallowing the sky.

Barnaby led me to his garage, which held an antique convertible Aston Martin.

"Whoa," I said. "We're going in this?"

"Sure are," Barnaby said, sliding in. "We've got some werewolf hunting to do."

"But isn't this, like, the most unsafe car ever?"

Barnaby laughed. "Just watch."

He fired up the engine and reversed the vehicle from the garage. Once we were clear of the ceiling, he shifted into *F*.

"F? What's that?"

Barnaby smirked. "Fly."

And so we did. We rose into the air and headed through the city. Now I loved riding my cast-iron skillet, but this was something different entirely. This was like being in *Back to the Future* or an even cooler movie that I hadn't seen yet.

"It's getting dark. I can't see below us," I said.

Barnaby flipped a switch, and floodlights lit the world below. I could see a good two hundred feet in front of us.

"Where do you think he is?" I said.

Barnaby tapped the steering wheel. "We're all creatures of habit, no matter who we are. As one of those, what place do you think the wolf knows best?"

I thought a moment. "The Cobweb Forest?"

Barnaby nodded. "That's what I think, too. Come on. Let's see if our hunch is correct."

"And you know how to use the stone to turn him back?"

Barnaby nodded. "That, I can do. What worries me is stopping him from killing us before I have a clean shot."

"I'll handle that part," I said. "I've communicated with him before. I know I can breach the werewolf's mind and touch Axel."

Barnaby squeezed my hand. "This is dangerous work. I'm grateful to you for helping."

I smiled. "I was about to say the same thing myself."

Within a couple of minutes the forest loomed ahead. The lights from town dimmed until only a few remained in sight while a sea of darkness faced us.

We headed toward the slab of concrete surrounded by tall hedges —the place where once a month Axel was chained and held until his night as a werewolf ended and he returned to normal.

Below, lights flared to life. Barnaby steered the car toward the copse of trees where shouting voices could now be heard.

"Get him! Hit him with that gun!"

Garrick's men had found the wolf first.

"Hurry," I said.

We rounded a copse of trees, and I saw them—two men and the

werewolf. The creature growled and snarled, sinking back on its haunches as if it was about to propel into an attack.

The car touched earth. Barnaby and I raced from the vehicle. We reached the men just as several figures popped into view.

Garrick and the rest of his team arrived as swirling mist that appeared among the trees. They must've been called in as backup.

The men raced toward Axel. Garrick had a different rifle this time, one that I feared might actually take the werewolf's life. Don't ask me what made me think that, maybe it was the ring of men with determined looks on their faces.

Or maybe it was the two silver shells I watched Garrick load into the rifle.

Yep, that was it.

I ran into the fray. "Stop!" I held out my hands, placing myself between the men and Axel. "We have a way to return him to normal. Put your weapons down!"

"Get out of there, Pepper," Garrick said. "He's wild now. Dangerous."

I didn't feel any fear when I turned to face the werewolf. The creature's dark eyes seemed filled with sadness as he gazed on me.

"Axel," I said. "I know you're in there. Talk to me."

I extended my hand, and once again the creature calmed. The growling and snarling stopped as he looked at me with curiosity. He leaned forward as if to sniff my hand and did.

Hot breath caressed my skin.

"Pepper," Garrick warned, "he hasn't hurt anyone yet, but if he touches you, I'll shoot him."

"Don't," I said.

The beast sniffed me for a moment and then lowered his head. I stroked the coarse fur. The creature quivered. His muscles trembled. He was scared. Whether it was Axel who was terrified or whether it was the creature, I didn't know. All I was certain of was that you get a group of men together to corner any living thing and that animal will be terrified. I know I would've been.

Then a single word flared in my head. The beast projected it there, and I knew it as plain as the nose on my face.

Help, he said.

The word crushed my heart but also made my chest swell. I could communicate with Axel in this form. He knew who and what he was, and he hadn't hurt anybody.

"Barnaby, are you ready?" I said softly, not wanting to startle the creature.

"Sure am," he said from behind me.

I heard Barnaby explain to Garrick. "I can return the wolf to his human form."

Garrick said, "Do it. Let's end this nightmare."

"We're going to turn you back," I said to the creature. "Hang on."

I tucked my hand to my side and stepped away, giving Barnaby the room he needed.

The werewolf kept a steady gaze on Barnaby as the wizard held the labradorite. Golden magic zoomed skyward from the stone as Barnaby spoke quietly.

The light flared up and then flew into the werewolf, encompassing him in a cocoon. The beast fought and snarled.

"Watch him, boys," Garrick said. "Get back."

We all shuffled back.

I reached out to him. "It's okay. No one's going to hurt you."

But he snarled more.

"What's going on?" I said to Barnaby.

"We're forcing transformation. It probably hurts."

I pressed my fingers to my forehead in worry. "Can you do anything to help?"

Barnaby shook his head. "It'll be over in a moment."

The werewolf continued to fight the magic, whirling on the men. He sank back on his haunches and lunged forward. Garrick lifted the shotgun and fired.

I screamed.

The wolf landed on the ground, unconscious. I rushed over to him.

The beast finally started to change, morphing back into Axel. The fur fell out, the bones shortened and his face shrank into the one I knew.

When he'd shifted completely, I noticed a small bullet wound in his shoulder.

Garrick strode over. "It's silver and will hurt him pretty bad if we don't get it out now." He turned to his men. "Come on! Let's get Axel to the doctor. There's not a minute to waste."

TWENTY-SEVEN

*I*t was two weeks later and a beautiful Saturday morning. Summer was finally retreating and cool autumn wind blew through Magnolia Cove. The leaves had started turning beautiful shades of amber and gold, and happiness buoyed in my chest as I strolled down Bubbling Cauldron on my way to open Familiar Place.

I unlocked the door with the golden key Uncle Donovan had sent me in the mail in a life that felt far, far away.

As soon as the door swung wide, the kittens meowed, the puppies barked and the birds chirped.

Feed us!

We're starving!

What took you so long?

I chuckled as I flipped light switches, topped off water bowls and filled food pans.

I had just turned the plastic window sign to OPEN when the bell above the door tinkled.

Axel strolled in, his left arm in a sling. "Morning." He placed a Styrofoam container on the counter.

I quirked a brow. "What's that?"

"Sweet tea for my sweet."

I laughed and stepped inside his single outstretched arm.

He pulled me in for a long kiss and hug. "I've missed you."

"You just saw me yesterday."

"Like I said, I've missed you."

I giggled. "How's the arm feel this morning?"

He rotated his shoulder. "Better. Doc says I'll be free of this sling in another week."

I clicked my tongue. "Betty offered to heal it for you."

When Axel shook his head, dark tendrils tumbled into his eyes. He raked them away. "Like I told you, I wanted to remember what happened. I want a reminder."

I shook my head. "I don't know why you're punishing yourself. It wasn't your fault."

He slumped back and leaned on the counter. "I know, but I need this."

I rubbed his good shoulder. "The community's behind you. No one was hurt."

"This time."

A flare of pain swelled in me. "We connected, Axel. I know you don't remember, but I spoke to the wolf and he responded. You're not completely lost when you become the beast."

He sighed.

I smiled. "I know you don't believe me, but it's true." A flicker of movement caught my gaze, and I glanced outside to see Barnaby Battle strolling down Bubbling Cauldron. "What happened with Delilah?"

Axel's blue eyes fixed on me. "She was sentenced today. After her full confession the judge didn't go easy on her—life in prison."

I grimaced. "She was a cold-blooded killer."

He nodded. "I never would've guessed. But anyway, she confessed to having an obsession with killing and enjoying it."

I pressed a finger to my lips. "And Samuel never told you who sneaked him into the Vault to steal the box?"

Axel shook his head. "Not directly, though if I had to guess, I'd say that Erasmus must've helped him in some way."

I quirked a brow. "Erasmus? But he's dedicated to keeping the contents safe."

"Doesn't mean the guardian doesn't prefer a little drama now and then."

"You've got a good point." Just then Erasmus passed in front of the store. "I guess he resigned from his post?"

"I think he's taking a sabbatical."

I clicked my tongue. "Can't say I blame him." I folded my arms and smiled at Axel. "I'm just glad you're okay."

He wrapped me in another hug and kissed my forehead. "And I feel the same about you." Axel studied me with those gorgeous blue eyes of his, and my heart ballooned. "You ready to get out of here tonight? Go on a real date?"

I exhaled. "So ready. Think we have to worry about Rufus?"

Axel chuckled. "From what you told me, I think Rufus'll leave you alone for a while. You gave that sorcerer a run for his money."

I smiled. "I'm finally getting the hang of these powers."

He brushed a strand of red hair from my eyes. "About time."

I swatted his chest.

"Ouch!"

"That didn't hurt. I missed your injured shoulder."

Axel kissed my lips again and headed toward the door. "See you in a few hours."

I waved and smiled. "Looking forward to it."

He blew me a kiss, which was like so seriously romantic. Yes, I was such a cheese ball that I caught it.

Axel disappeared, and I stood in the still silence for a few minutes, ruminating on how much he meant to me and how happy I was that when he'd come to and realized the havoc he'd created in town while loose in his wolf form, that Axel hadn't brooded about it. He took it with his chin up, relieved that no one had been hurt and thankful that the police had been willing to take him down but hadn't.

And so the question remained—had it been the silver bullet that changed him back, or the labradorite?

We'd never know, but it didn't matter. Axel was himself, Rufus was beaten back to whatever hole he'd crawled out of, and the killer had been caught.

Whew. All in a week's work.

A scraping from the rear of the store caught my attention. It sounded like someone entering the back door, but that was impossible. I was the only person with a key.

Concerned, I stepped into the hall. Sure enough, the doorknob turned as if someone was about to enter.

Then they did. A man stumbled through, a golden key that matched mine in his hand.

He had thinning white hair and oval spectacles resting on his nose. I instantly recognized him.

"Uncle Donovan," I said, reaching for him.

My supposed-to-be-dead uncle fell to his knees. I wrapped my arms around him, barely processing what was happening.

"Uncle?" I repeated, confused as heck and unsure if this was a ghost or a man I was touching.

Donovan stared ahead for a moment before blinking at me. His eyes seemed to focus, and his head jerked. "Pepper! Thank goodness you're here."

"What's going on?"

Donovan heaved himself off the floor and grabbed my arms. "Pepper. I'm in grave danger. I'm afraid you might be, too. I need your help if we're both going to survive what's coming."

I nearly slapped my forehead. Oh boy, here we go again.

ALSO BY AMY BOYLES

SWEET TEA WICH MYSTERIES
SOUTHERN MAGIC
SOUTHERN SPELLS
SOUTHERN MYTHS
SOUTHERN SORCERY
SOUTHERN CURSES
SOUTHERN KARMA

BLESS YOUR WITCH SERIES
SCARED WITCHLESS
KISS MY WITCH
QUEEN WITCH
QUIT YOUR WITCHIN'
FOR WITCH'S SAKE
DON'T GIVE A WITCH
WITCH MY GRITS
FRIED GREEN WITCH
SOUTHERN WITCHING
Y'ALL WITCHES
HOLD YOUR WITCHES

SOUTHERN SINGLE MOM PARANORMAL MYSTERIES
The Witch's Handbook to Hunting Vampires
The Witch's Handbook to Catching Werewolves
The Witch's Handbook to Trapping Demons

ABOUT THE AUTHOR

Amy Boyles grew up reading Judy Blume and Christopher Pike. Somehow, the combination of coming of age books and teenage murder mysteries made her want to be a writer. After graduating college at DePauw University, she spent some time living in Chicago, Louisville, and New York before settling back in the South. Now, she spends her time chasing two preschoolers while trying to stir up trouble in Silver Springs, Alabama, the fictional town where Dylan Apel and her sisters are trying to master witchcraft, tame their crazy relatives, and juggle their love lives. She loves to hear from readers! You can email her at amy@amyboylesauthor.com.

CPSIA information can be obtained
at www.ICGtesting.com
Printed in the USA
LVHW040347010523
745726LV00013B/111